GIRL WITH A VIOLIN

A Psychological Thriller

What People Are Saying About
GIRL WITH A VIOLIN

"From the first paragraph, the reader's curiosity is immediately piqued, and the adventure begins. Bartlett takes us on a musical journey worthy of the most complicated composition, and on the way, we meet a cast of characters that makes us want to pick up an instrument and join the band.

"The hallmark of a great mystery/psychological thriller is to keep the reader guessing. Bartlett does this, but with a twist. The book starts out as a mystery but becomes a psychological thriller that will not disappoint.

"I can't wait for her next book!"
—Helen Cameron, PhD, Higher Education Administration

"I liked Bartlett's book a lot and would recommend it to anyone who is interested in the tightknit conversations that happens among musical friends.

"I am a fellow musician and well acquainted with both bluegrass and folk music genres. I enjoyed *Girl with a Violin* and found that, as a musician, it perked along quite well. Wendy is spot on target with her characterizations of her musicians. We musicians are a narcissistic and competitive bunch as individuals, but also tribal by necessity."
—Mike Mirabella, singer-songwriter and author of *On the Luck of an Irish Sailor* and *Sister Butterfly*, the first in The Carla Series. *I Used to be Shy* (the second in the series) is coming in 2022.

GIRL WITH A VIOLIN

A Psychological Thriller

Best wishes in London 2022
Wendy Bartlett

WENDY BARTLETT

San Francisco Writers Conference Award Winner

Kensington Hill Books
Berkeley, California

Kensington Hill Books
Berkeley, California

kensingtonhillbooks.com

Girl with a Violin: A Psychological Thriller
/ Wendy Bartlett
ISBN 978-1-944907-21-1 print
ISBN 978-1-944907-20-4 ebook
Library of Congress Control Number: 2021924297

*This book is dedicated to
all musicians. Everywhere.*

ACKNOWLEDGMENTS

These people have all contributed in their unique ways to make this novel what it is: Helen Holt, Charlie Hopper, Harry Starkey-Midah, Phil Pesch, Joe Miller, John Cooke, Angie Powers, Elizabeth Stark, Helen Cameron, Michael Mirabella, Peggy Newgarden and Jude Reseigne.

Thanks for my eternally patient writers' group: Joyce Scott, Marilynn Rowland, Sarita James, Dean Curtis, and Ruth Hanham. Thanks to Tyra Gilb and Jane Brodie for thoughtful cover ideas. Special thanks to Ruth Schwartz for her awesome cover design and her amazing publishing help. And to the BAIPA group, who listened to me for years!

A special shout out to Ken Sherman, L.A. agent, for pointing his finger at me after I pitched my novel as a possible movie, and saying, "Now, THAT'S a movie!"

I also want to acknowledge the following folks for their incredible work on the audio play version of this book: Becky Parker Geist, all the actors and singers, and Findaway Audio Voices; Lee Corbie-Wells, Marc Silber and Jude Reseigne for their original music and songs; Paul Lynch for advice and music research; Joe Miller for musical ideas; David Colin Carr for editing and for recommending Ken Sherman. I would also like to thank John Orland for showing me how to use Final Draft.

THE KIDNAPPER

The kidnapper remains calm and plays his guitar so well, so passionately that night, that not one of the musicians will think for a moment that, as he strums, he is making his plans for Beau's abduction.

The first part of his plan is to remain sober, so that, while everybody else is stoned and drunk, it all goes off perfectly.

The crowd mutters as they are scattered among the sofas, chairs and coffee tables in their Sierra Mansion, still cluttered with empty bottles. The kidnapper plays on and on. Sometimes a burst of clapping develops, as eighteen-year-old Beau soars to musical heights with her furiously fast arpeggios up and down the strings. They play as if they have rehearsed forever, and yet it is, as usual, off the cuff, solidified by each one's enormous past of competitions won and hours of study. People know the brilliant ones are forced to be in the company of enthusiastic, yet imperfect players, strumming quietly, struggling with fast-changing bar chords, sometimes lagging a beat or two behind, and the relentless fast pace of the fiddlers and bluegrass banjo players. The kidnapper enjoys this moment, this camaraderie, this heart-racing rush to the climactic ending.

The kidnapper's beer bottle remains full. He pretends to take a swig occasionally but manages to block its entrance into his throat with his tongue.

His mind begins to grind again, as he smiles and holds up his palm for a high five with Beau, who is eighteen today.

"Have another drink," he offers.

"No, that's okay. I've had too many already. Birthday girl and all that! Yes!" She stretches out her hand to wave and he puts a bottle in her hand anyway. She takes another swig before putting the bottle down.

He goes over his plans as he tunes his guitar to perfect pitch.

ABDUCTION

The moon shines down the long, curved dirt driveway and silhouettes the black-shadowed pine treetops. Beau peers out of the large window and, feeling strangely dizzy and unaware that she is now high on something the kidnapper has just added to her drink, she leaves her fiddle in its stand, kisses her boyfriend, Tiger, goodbye, while he is in the middle of singing a great song, and staggers outside to see the stars.

Her knuckles feel raw from holding her bow in one hand and her precious violin in the other for six hours. She looks up, her eyes lazily crossing inwards as the sky and stars above spin, and then gravity pulls her floating body down hard onto the driveway gravel. From her hands and knees, she pushes against the sharp stones and tries to get up. Yet, no matter how she struggles to rise, her world swirls like she is on a cascading boat in a storm, and she falls back down, bumping her cheek on the ground. Her eyelids, heavy and drooping, close like a fade-out at the end of a movie.

In her muddled state, Beau barely hears the crunch of footsteps approaching from behind her. Wobbling, she manages to stand up, but then a cloth covers her nose and mouth, and duct tape is slapped over the cloth in her mouth. Her arm is twisted so firmly that she can't turn around to see who is doing this, and then a blindfold is slipped over her eyes. Whatever movement she makes pulls her arm muscles taut and makes them scream with pain. She is terrified and the fire in her arm informs her that this is not some prankster. Her hand is going limp, but still she punches at him in her dizzy state. Her fingers get caught in the pocket of her shorts and it tears. Whoever it is clasps both of her hands and ties her wrists behind her with something that feels like a rope, then wraps her ankles with it. He grabs around her waist and heaves her slight frame up onto his shoulders.

She begins to lose consciousness. The world is circling. She feels sick as he strides down the driveway without a word. Her head is foggy. Her eyes feel like they are popping out. Her arms sting from his firm grip on them.

Beau fades in and out of consciousness. *Will I be killed, slowly, painfully? Where is he taking me? Down the mountain?* After walking with her for only a few minutes, he slides her almost gently onto the cold ground. He unties her wrists, then binds her wrists together in front. She tries to hit him. She lies there, squirming and kicking. Maybe, just maybe, all this is a foggy moment of her middle-of-the-night last deep hit of pot. She screams inside her head! *Will he now rape me? Will he cut me up or shoot me?*

But then she hears her abductor melting into the distance. The night noises sift into her consciousness. There is a musty scent of pot, but it might be her breath. Her brain churns through all the musicians, but her mind is sloshing like water and her eyes are stinging from the horrible chloroform smell.

Moaning only blocks her breathing. Her arms ache from being twisted and she fades again into nothingness.

When she comes to, Beau sniffs like a dog trying to figure out the scent of this person; trying to recognize this smell that she has never consciously noticed before. All she smells is something like pot and a sickening smell like cleaning ammonia that makes her gag, contrasting with the sweet scent of the pine trees around her.

She slumps into herself and can't think—can't think at all. While she wonders what might happen next, she can hear the distant music she loves so much. She hears the subtle, yet familiar, noises of the night. After a while, she fears that she has just been left all alone to die in the forest with the night animals.

Frightened and nauseous, Beau remembers all the news programs she's seen with Tiger, of people in dire situations that would never, ever happen to her. She tries to remember who was near her just as she was attacked. But she cannot even remember if she was outside or inside just before her mouth was covered.

For a long time, Beau can't move. Her wrists are burning from the rope. She wiggles her jaw to loosen the tape. Her legs, stretched out before her, feel like two heavy men are sitting on them.

It doesn't help that Beau can hear Tiger twanging away up at the Mansion on her favorite song, "*You settle down and stay with the one who loves you.*" She can just make out the lyrics from this distance, but she knows them well. She always takes a solo right about now. Surely, he will wonder why she has not appeared, breathless, fiddle under her chin, with her bow at the ready? Perhaps he is singing this song just now to draw her back from her upstairs bedroom? After all, she usually stays up until dawn at these jam sessions. Doesn't he notice she has not really said goodnight?

Her wild imagination clings onto the distant notes and she imagines her arms holding the fiddle under her chin; her eyes close as she touches the strings lightly, up and down the neck like a hummingbird. This fantasy calms her down. But as her mind races between the notes, her cramped body, chilly on the ground, sinks like an anchor into the cold earth. The night sounds of the forest above her and around her creep into her ear, diminishing her fantasized notes, drowning out her musings that this must be a practical joke, and that any moment she will be set free with some drunken idiot saying, 'fooled you!'

Something touches her left ear. All her attention is right there. Then it is gone. Now it is moving over her ribs: it slithers. She freezes. She remembers that rattlesnakes like this altitude in the summer. She holds very still: she begins to think of her mantra that she has not said in years—*Om. Om.* The snake's movement across her waist almost tickles. It moves around and around and, clearly, it is camping on her waist, and a horrible feeling of a feathery lump becomes heavy — very heavy. She can hardly breathe.

Beau's limbs ache. She imagines a flashing tongue flipping from the snake's mouth. Her body starts shivering against her will. The snake wiggles, and then stops moving. Is it preparing its poison? Might it move away as easily as it has come? *Oh, why doesn't somebody come and save me?*

Her fuzzy mind churns through all the musicians and she wonders which one would want to treat her this way. Up to now, she has always felt loved, or at least admired. It seems like everybody loves her — well, except a few jealous girls who struggle with their three chords and weak voices.

Beau couldn't have talked this person out of anything once he taped her mouth shut. Her mind scatters through every possibility: who did this to her? She feels her legs stiffening as she lies there, wherever she is, and works her tongue like a reptile against the cloth held down by the tape across her mouth. She feels her whole upper body shaking!

As the faint light of a new day creeps through her blindfold and under her head cover, the serpent begins to uncoil. It slithers off her body — so lightly, so innocently — to go on with the business of survival, no doubt away from her. But then it circles back towards her head and the weight of its long body is curving along her neck. Now the whole serpent is relaxing on her neck, and a muffled rattling sound right next to her ear announces its owner's power.

PURE, PURE LOVE!

Distant music filters in and out of Beau's brain like a radio left on. The driving beat of a bluegrass banjo flutters by. She would have joined in right this minute. Her chin would have been holding her fiddle, her bow perched on the strings, her body standing freely. Ralph, the old hippie, in spite of his age, will be doing the jig around the room while Martin will be revving up to the beat of the music and Don, Beau's father, will hold the piece together with his bass.

Millie's dad, Jim, will be keeping a steady drumbeat, and Will is probably leaning into his harmonica like a giraffe finding a tasty leaf on a lower branch while he blows in and out effortlessly. As she lies there, so cold and helpless, longing to hum along, yet so little air returns to push notes into life and she is left a lonely dreamer.

Beau doesn't want this dream to end. If it ends, she will be here, lying on the cold earth, tied and bound, a chill running down her back. She hears only the animals searching through the dry pine nettles for food, her muscles so tight like a taut string ready to bust, the snake resting on her neck, and the kidnapper perhaps awakening to the dawn chorus and now ready to do the deed: the horrible deed. *Oh, please, let me back into my orchestra! Even those really old players and mom's banjo; cozy around in a circle, people unafraid, beyond showing off, just swaying with the lifting notes for love, not adulation, just pure love. Pure, pure love!*

There is no wind. Beau realizes from sniffing the air that she is most likely in a shallow hole she knows so well from her childhood. She shivers frequently, listening for any sounds she can make out. The sudden stillness is eerie.

Beau can hear only her own breathing now. It is slowing down. She decides she will not allow herself to go back to sleep. She wiggles her tongue and tries to clear her dry throat. Her tongue pushes at the cloth. It begins to loosen a little more. She closes her eyes, catching herself drifting off, then purposely opens her eyes a little, feeling the blindfold against her eyelids. She stops her tongue from pushing against the wet cloth and listens like she is almost deaf. She begins again; she gags; she feels sick. She consciously relaxes her tongue and tries to get more air in through her nostrils.

Beau drifts in and out of slumber, and now the chirping of the jays high in the pines is dissolving the silent night. There is a certain cadence of the sounds, one chirp against another. *Nobody is coming back. Have I been forgotten?* The snake still sleeps like an arm on her neck. She dare not move.

Beau tries once again to wiggle her wrists out of their binding. It is pointless. Whoever tied these knots must have been a sailor. Who does she know who is a sailor? Who sings sea shanties? Oh, now she really feels nuts! *Does everything have to tie into my music?*

As dawn turns into day, she begins to think she has been abandoned. She so dreads the kidnapper's return, yet wonders why he hasn't come back during those long, cold hours. She actually begins to hope he will arrive shortly, just to know he has not left her there to die. She feels confused and guilty even entertaining this horrible thought. *Am I going crazy? Is this what the end of my life is going to be? Is this the end of my career? Have I practiced for thousands of hours, only to be left alone in this cold and damp hole on the mountainside?*

MOONBEAM

Sometime after 3 AM, on his way back outside with the hardest part of his abduction done, the kidnapper is hoodwinked by Beau's friend, Moonbeam, into taking a drink of fizzy water before he gets to the door. He drinks it to humor her. For fun, she has dissolved several Quaaludes in the water and now the kidnapper is staggering around the living room while she giggles. Within minutes, he falls face down onto the couch. He struggles to get up. *Beau is tied up and hidden.* His whole body is stone; his eyelids shut. His mind reels and he forgets what he is planning to do. He lies there, paralyzed, and then he passes out. Most of the older players gradually disappear back into their tents and vans.

In the morning, the kidnapper wakes up. The light stabs his pupils; his back feels like a split log; his lower lip is swollen as if he has fallen onto something hard. He struggles to his feet and scans the room for his guitar and fiddle. His guitar is as he left it; his fiddle is in its case.

What in the world has happened to him? He feels strange and disoriented. Right away, he imagines he has been drugged. But by whom? He is furious. *Beau is still out there, tied up.*

He sticks his jaw out and stretches his neck and looks around at the other sleeping figures lying around the floor and on the couches: Ted grasping his fiddle with a contented smile; Chuck flat on his back with his mouth wide open and Paul in a fetal position, still grasping a beer bottle in one hand and his harmonica in the other.

The kidnapper gets up too quickly and bumps his head on a standing lamp with a stained-glass shade. "Damn!" he mutters. He begins to weave through the sleeping bodies. It is still very early. Hopefully, no one will see him leave and get curious. *Who the hell has done this to me?*

He hears two people whispering in the large kitchen. If he slips out right now, nobody will see him. The door is ajar and beckoning to him. His weary eyes lead his aching head and body towards the door, which feels like it is across an interminable stage. After only one more step he will be free of any witnesses.

"Morning," says Don, yawning and shuffling towards the kitchen. Maybe Don will keep going, since he has just awakened and has probably not had coffee. But the kidnapper sees that apparently, he has already had coffee. At least he is starting a conversation that only sounds like a series of complaints, a gibberish that is probably not meant to be heard, unless one has already had coffee, too.

"Got a hangover," Don says.

"Yep. Me, too!"

Don comes to a slow halt and surveys the mess of empty beer bottles and red paper plates with countless green and brown leftovers on the dining table and the coffee tables.

"Gonna have to have a cleanup party," Don mutters.

"Yep."

"Same drill. Gotta watch out for the slackers: we know who they are."

"We do," says the kidnapper.

"Coffee?" Don asks.

The kidnapper sees that he is not going to be able to slip away right now. He will move Beau later. *Damned daylight!*

They shuffle towards the kitchen, kicking away the bottles left on the floor.

GOODBYE WITH A KISS

Despite the early hour, the music begins. After the coffee wakes them up, a vibrant display of virtuosity inevitably shoots from one musician to the next around the giant living room. As soon as the banjo takes off, the mandolin's rapid-fire melody brings out Misty on the clarinet with Gershwin sounds that challenge Marvin on the fiddle to a pitch and degree of skill that is almost inborn, like a bird's song. The guitar players charge up and down their fretboards with complicated finger patterns and wide stretches of their little fingers that almost hurt to watch. Their fingerpicking chooses notes in a way that challenge, yet parallel, the rapid notes of Jim on the mandolin. In the corner, Charlie, on his box drum, keeps a hypnotic beat going so that its rhythm holds this enthusiastic group together so they will not take off, tumbling and flying out the double doors into the tops of the pine trees.

No one is willing to stop. With the increased confidence and competitive nature of these players, it is an endless challenge to make each instrumental verse more complicated than the previous one.

Millie, Beau's mother, can play her banjo the fastest and in her sleep, but one part of her mind that isn't on automatic is reserved for a digging concern: why hasn't Beau come back and joined in? Where did Beau sleep? Why is her cell phone plugged in on the dinner table? Why did she leave her violin so carelessly on her stand, as if she had only left it for a moment?

It is Millie's time to shine, and she does so while the younger banjo players watch like ravens, trying to figure out how she gets her fingers to move like a whirlwind. At the end of the piece, everybody laughs at the beauty of the music they have created.

As she plays, Millie thinks about Tiger, Beau's boyfriend. He hasn't come in to play yet. The guy is handsome with dark hair. He plays the guitar so fast that both hands become a blur. Just listening is awe-inspiring, the melody singing out, entwined with the flowing bass notes and trills. He has a swagger that says it all. He is no cowboy, but you can imagine his holster and guns and a belt full of shiny bullets around his waist. He wears a cowboy hat so much he only gets tanned on his chin and neck. He leans against the bar in the large living room like he is in the movies. He slides his empty glass down the proverbial counter and says, "Same again," without so much as a please or thank you.

Millie always keeps a beady eye on him with her precious Beau. He'd better treat her like gold, or Millie will not play her banjo with him, or worse.

Millie and Tiger played up a storm last night. She casts her eyes down as she tears across her banjo strings. Someone had better figure out where Beau is, or they will all be detectives that day instead of warmed-up musicians and frog-like singers.

OBEY

Sad in the boy's throat; sad in the tears that threaten to swell at the corner of his eyes; sad because he can't really know where it all is coming from, just emerging from a hidden cavern in his gut, once so protected, where now, the layers diminish and the wound surfaces to the touch, where the body sheds its defenses. That sad place that started him hiding at age five under the covers in choked, lonely sobs, or behind a stoic face and a sturdy stance. Blinking eyes, lowered for more than privacy, lowered for fear of another exposure to a harsh, uncaring world, seem to peel the flesh back where the wound is exposed to oxygen; germs, bacteria; noise.

He sinks, he sinks; he tries the old methods, but nothing covers him up, nothing protects him. Shivering and shaking, his knees knock, his lower lip and his cheeks quiver. He stands there, psychologically naked, vulnerable, imaginary hands covering his private parts only hidden by a frail cloth of woolen shorts. Yes, sir, yes, sir, he says, and his stomach rumbles like a washing machine and he dies again.

He must run, but he must stand there and obey his father's commands, his anger, his disappointment, with his mother, standing just behind his father, full of her own brand of disillusion. Sad the boy is,

13

water running from his nose, his obligatory handkerchief falling to the cold floor. He may not lean down to retrieve it; he must stand and feel the cruel trickle under his nose as it runs over his lips and drips onto the polished floor.

He wheezes, he shudders, the Professor nods and the boy runs. They know where he is running. They know, and it's not their fault. It is his. They are right and innocent, while he is their only child (once their supreme joy), but now their biggest disappointment. The boy cannot bear it, but he must — he must play his violin better.

He can do that. He will play better; he will spend more hours with his bow across the strings, and he will stand the whole time and play the beauty that Brahms and Vivaldi wrote for him. He is Vivaldi; he is Brahms; he is Bach. Weren't they once five years old? Were they ever a disappointing kid who then made good when they were older? Were they sad, too? He will never know. He sees their beautiful notes strung together as he raises his bow and holds his violin like an appendage and begins again. He will be perfect. Can he be even more perfect? Will his tears go away, and will they love him like they used to?

The record is set: It spins and the invention of a needle together with the record pours out his orchestra and he plays with the greatest musicians. He is tiny, and he is sad, and he knows he is becoming one of the greatest. He will try harder.

He loves his music. He hates his parents! He hates them! He wants to kill them! They don't love him. He will try harder. He will cry more, but alone; so alone, in his bedroom where echoes of his notes will filter down the hallway and the grand staircase and maybe into the parlor. The doors are always open; the ears are listening. He feels the pride of their nodding as he pleases them from afar. His tears subside and he secretly knows they might still have hope for him. But how can he play better? He can't! He can't!

Sunday Morning: Gone

Now Millie is sitting by the unopened Sunday edition of the *San Francisco Chronicle*, her eyes bleary, her banjo in its stand by her side. Six hours of sleep is fine once a month, but two nights running…she can understand her father's hangover. How can she read the paper with Beau still not turning up?

Jim, Millie's father frequently has his guitar strapped around his shoulders, and if he has developed a potbelly over the years, it is tidily hidden by this constant appendage.

"Beau is an independent girl," he says. "If she decided to take off in the middle of the night, it normally wouldn't be a worry for us—we might do the same thing ourselves—but at her own birthday party, and alone?" He walks over to Millie. "Where'd she say she was going?"

"She didn't tell me, Dad. Didn't take her truck."

"Or her phone. It's on the kitchen table."

"Leave it there," Millie says, lifting the coffee pot over Don's cup. "It might ring."

Millie pours a cup of coffee for Don in his favorite large blue cup. She scraps her plan to finish her recent landscape painting later.

"Should we worry?" asks Jim.

"It's strange. I'm not sure. Who else left the party?"

Both of Beau's parents bow their heads and rub their brows. Don reaches over and pulls a cigarette out and lights it. Millie looks at him and frowns. Neither can think of anybody who wanted to leave. A lot of the fun is staying overnight.

Four younger musicians straggle in, bleary from almost no sleep, but ready to start the music up after a couple of cups of coffee. Young Tiger pries his eyes open and looks around the large central kitchen. He grabs a red mug from a hook under the cupboard and shuffles over to the coffee pot and pours, listening as the sound gurgles and stops. He picks up the cup and looks around. They are all staring at him.

He looks at Millie now. "What?" he says, coffee cup halfway to his lips.

Silence. "What? Why the looks?"

Most of the coffee drinkers turn away.

"Hey, I know I was too loud last night; well, this morning. Probably woke you up." He takes a sip. "Hey, where's Beau?"

They look back at his young, wasted, stubbly face.

"She's gone," Millie says, wiping her hands on her jeans.

"Gone? Where'd she go?" Tiger licks his mustache and saunters over to the gigantic knotty pine table, pulls out a chair and sits down. He fumbles for his cigarettes.

"She's disappeared," Jim says. "You know where she went?"

"Hell, no! What'd she go and do that for? I saw her truck. Must be in one of those bedrooms upstairs. I'll take a look after my coffee."

"We thought she would have been with you," Don says.

"Naw," says Tiger. "I flaked on the couch about two hours ago. Couldn't have climbed the stairs if my life depended on it." He chuckles to himself. "Stoned blind," he adds. "Good music, wasn't it?"

"Yep," Don says. "Always the best at the end when the good ones are left, and the egos have gone hoarse and sacked out."

"Yep," they all say, except Millie who went to bed by 1 AM and doesn't think she has an ego problem. Her banjo playing is outstanding: everybody says so. And she thinks she is the lowest rung of ego walking around that ranch.

But Beau and her friends have voices like angels. They show off their high notes like they are birds singing at the tops of the trees and no one can reach them. The older musicians admire them; some are jealous of them. *These young people are taking over.* The young musicians pant for their own emerging moments. You can hear them scratching the dirt with their front paws, head to ground; eyes front; ready to boot those old croaking singers out of the ballpark. *And those songs*, the older ones think. *So slow, no beat! How can you dance to that?*

Tiger finishes his coffee and wanders over to get his guitar. He looks towards the door, shrugs his shoulders, and picks it up. Before he went to the kitchen, he'd already made an effort to check in her bedroom. Beau often disappeared somewhere—just liked being alone sometimes. Beau will surface soon. Don gives him a look.

"Maybe this is serious," Don says.

"Naw!" Tiger looks up while singing quietly and starting to strum his guitar. "She's just doing her thing."

Millie gives Tiger a dirty look.

"Oh, hell!" Tiger says, stopping his song in the middle. "I'll go find her."

"When did you last see her?" asks Millie.

"Huh? Sometime in the night. I don't remember. I think she kissed my neck somewhere during a quiet ballad. Now I remember. I couldn't stop in the middle of the song to ask her where she was going. At least she said goodbye with a kiss. Let me go find her. Can't be that far."

"Suit yourself. We've looked everywhere in the house," Millie says, settling her banjo back into its cradle. "I'm calling the sheriff."

"Good idea," Don says.

Tiger dashes out of the room, pausing to light his cigarette. "Damned lighter never works." He turns out of the kitchen and heads outside.

SHE'LL TURN UP

"Going outside," Martin mumbles, walking through the doors that lead to the deck, on Tiger's heels. They go down the wide, wooden stairs to keep the smoke away from the others, as per the house rules.

Don appears at the opened double doors. "Beau's still missing!"

"I'm going to try to find her again," Tiger says, slowing his pace. "I bet she's just sleeping it off somewhere."

"Nope," says Don, on his way to the stairs.

"Must be right here on the property somewhere," Martin says to Tiger. "Maybe in someone's tent, or maybe in an RV."

Tiger stops and thinks for a moment, then draws in the nicotine Beau so hates. Martin looks out at the pine trees and sky.

"Naw," says Tiger. "What would she do that for? She has a great bedroom. She knows this land so well she probably never wants to walk all over it again. Eighty acres! That's for ten-year-olds. Naw. The big city is more likely for her. But where would she go without *moi?*"

Martin smiles and pulls out his pot stash. Don wanders over to Martin.

"You have a sixth sense for pot," Martin says.

"Oh, really? I had no idea. Honest!" says Don.

Tiger blows out a smoke ring and stubs out his cigarette on the large stone at his feet. "What do you think, Don?"

"You'd think I would know her well enough, but she gave no hint. She seemed so pleased with this whole party idea. Maybe she's got those female blues," says Don.

They all chuckle and Martin inhales, with his chest pushing outwards, and holds his breath as he passes the joint to Don.

"I know she loves us, even though she left home at fifteen. She has her own trajectory," Don says.

"How's the music scene in San Francisco, Tiger?" Martin asks.

"I've got to go find her," says Tiger, adding, "Music scene for her or what?"

"Yeah. Is she happy enough with Celtic and bluegrass, for instance?"

"Seems fine. Never better. She's been taking an opera history class, but nothing too exciting. Hardly mentions it. Just trying to stack up units."

"Two years done and only eighteen, young enough to spread her wings and become an opera singer," Martin says, while holding his breath.

"Not in a million years!" Tiger says, turning his back and starting to jog away.

"Isn't she taking classical theory?" Martin asks, exhaling.

"Who knows," Tiger says. "She's unpredictable, you know that."

"You can say that again," Don says, reaching for what's left of the joint.

Tiger swings back around with his hand out for a final drag from Don. The joint is circulating, diminishing into a tiny stub.

Millie arrives at the double doors. "You all figured out the state of the world yet?"

Martin and Don turn around, both leaning back on the railing.

"Almost, my dear one," says Don.

"Just going to find her, can't be far," says Tiger, handing the roach back to Don and swiftly striding away.

Martin brushes the sides of his jeans and says, "Guess we'd better try looking for her again."

"All the vans, tents and cabins have been checked," says Millie. "Not a trace."

The men look at her face. She's a brave woman, but her lower lip is quivering, and her right eyelid is twitching.

Martin climbs up the wooden stairs to the deck and goes to put his arm around her. "Not to worry, Millie. We'll find her."

STILL TOGETHER

Tiger gets away from Martin and Don but is not sure where to look He doesn't get further than the shadiest deck on the other side of the house, the smokers' deck, where he lights yet another cigarette. George joins him.

"Morning," grunts George. Jim's buddy, George, is in his seventies and still smoking a pack a day, determined to beat the odds. His singing voice is shot, so he pretends to be Dylan and speaks a lot of the lyrics, especially the high notes. George also mostly carries his mandolin strapped to his back after someone sat on his last one at a jam in San Francisco.

"Beau's disappeared," Tiger says.

"I heard. Should we be worried?"

"Naw. She's always doing that. Trouble is, nobody seems to know where she went."

"You should! You're still together, aren't you?"

"Well, yes and no," says Tiger. "She can't stand my smoking much anymore. Never mentioned it when we got together last year! Now she's coughing all the time. She slept somewhere last night. But I was awake almost all night. Never saw her after about 2 AM."

"Well, that's hopeful. At least she was around until 2 AM."

Tiger stubs out his cigarette. "Yeah. She probably crashed some-where and is still sleeping. I just passed out in the living room."

"So, are we worrying, to quote Don?" George asks.

"Naw. She'll turn up when she hears our music. She can't resist star power with that fiddle!"

"Well, she's a real star, Tiger. That young lady is full of a talent few people are given. Seen Ralph this morning?"

"Can't remember. Going back in right now."

Tiger smiles, looks around for signs of Beau, then scuffs back to-wards the kitchen. Several more sleepy musicians are standing around sipping coffee. Millie is making a new pot.

"Thought you were out looking for Beau," Don says.

"I got waylaid," Tiger says. "Talking with George, the man of wis-dom himself. I figured we could start back up playing. That way she'll turn up after that no matter how tired she is."

Don frowns.

"Who's ready for more coffee?" Millie says.

George strides in and begins playing his mandolin. Within thirty seconds, a harmonica chimes in from the next room. A guitar strums along and Millie eyes her banjo and wonders if she plays really loudly, if, indeed, Beau will finally surface, fiddle in hand.

Suspects

Millie sits at the end of the long wooden table, making her list with the stub of a pencil while the rest of the musicians sip their coffee. *It will not be long until Beau turns up. Beau is probably perfectly fine.* And yet, as time wears away, Millie's suspicious brain keeps thinking there might be foul play. Maybe some jerk is jealous: jealous of a brilliant violinist stepping into the limelight that was once held by an older folksinging star. Jealousy could also extend to Beau's relationship with Tiger. Just think of all those young girls who claim to love him. Two successful musicians, Tiger and Beau, hogging the show: young, energetic, playing all night long and up early to begin playing again.

Millie scratches three new hairs sprouting on her chin. Who would be so jealous? Her busy mind files through all the aging performers who were stars in their youth, whose tips are dwindling, and whose audience is politely clapping. Millie even thinks of herself and laughs: her banjo picking is legendary by now. No one can touch her. She leans back in her security and crosses her own ego off the list.

Millie jots down a few more names, including some of the older men who'd begun coughing too often and couldn't sustain a musical note. Before she realizes it, Millie's list has grown so long that she understands that it includes everybody who was at the jam. But try as she does, she can't quite draw a line of innocence through anyone's name except her own. She knows she isn't the culprit. But she guiltily wonders even about Don. He has those jealous tendencies. He is just old enough to cover them up with a joke or change the subject with a new song. *But Don wouldn't hurt his own daughter!* Was she going crazy? What was she thinking? She draws a dark, thick line through his name.

Then Millie remembers one more person—a guy—great violin player though he'd stuck to the lead guitar most of last night. He is new: what's his name? Don is sitting just outside on the deck.

"Don—what's the name of that new guy?" she yells.

"What new guy?" he yells back. "Oh! That bass player who hogged every group he floated to? His name is Ranger. Wasn't he hanging around Beau? Whenever she changed groups, there he was, moseying over like he owned her. Where'd he sleep, anyway?"

Everybody looks up from their instruments and shrugs.

And where is he now?

There is an awful lull in the music as dozens of bleary eyes look around them and see nobody resembling Ranger in his cowboy hat with that stupid red and black feather. *Bird killer.* And those yellow fingers. Another cigarette smoker! And those missing teeth!

"Oh, that guy who held on to that eternal cigarette that he swore wasn't lit? I think he had a cup of coffee about twenty minutes ago," says Millie. *No smoking of any kind in the house,* her sign says at the front door.

Several older musicians wander in, yawning.

"Morning," says that very man, hat half covering his shifty eyes, making his way once again towards the coffee pot.

Helping himself to a second cup of coffee causes some shuffling and a little elbowing. No, this new guy doesn't know the rules. You have to check that everybody else gets firsts! He rubs the stubble on his chin and pours his coffee like nobody is measuring him up over the rims of their own cups.

The music slows to a stop. All eyes are on him. The quiet is too much for Millie.

"Sleep okay?" she asks the interloper. He puts some cream into his coffee, oblivious to her comment. As he turns around and raises it to his lips, he sees all those accusing eyes. Where is the joviality of the night, the stars, the moon, just now?

"What?" Ranger says to nobody.

"Did you sleep well?" Millie asks again.

"Oh, me? Yes, I did. Yes, I did."

"Where?"

"Where?"

"Did you find a good couch or a hammock?"

"Ah! No. I just slumped right down on the deck. I think I was the last one standing. It must've been 4 AM."

"Who were you playing with at that hour?" Don asks, trying not to sound too curious or interested.

"Darned if I know. I drank too much to see straight if you must know."

Millie decides not to cross him off the list.

DIFFERENT PARENTS

Beau is sinking into her situation like a rock tossed into the ocean. Life is unfair. Practicing for hours a day since forever and she isn't all that sure she wants to be such a brilliant fiddler.

Maybe with different parents, not folkie types, she would have soared to concertmaster in a symphony orchestra. Why do her parents have such power over her? What if she had been born into a completely different family, or even in a different country? Who would she be? Perhaps her voice would have been guided into opera. Maybe her fiddle playing would be like Paganini rather than Alison Krauss. Maybe her parents wouldn't have been so lame. Even her mom was an overbearing nuisance.

In her dreamy imagination Beau senses a crowd of musicians around her looking down into the shallow hole, staring in: *You should have listened to me. You should have stayed closer to Tiger. You shouldn't act so free. You're small. You're unbearable. Don't take liberation so far. Do as we do. We know,* they said, leaning over her covered face. *You probably were asking for it. At least you look down and don't smile too much. Dance, child! Stamp your feet! Bring out the Irish! Enjoy! Stop looking so serious.*

The imaginary faces look mean. They don't love her. They own her. Beau never wants to play music again. It's fun being famous, that's for sure. They just want to touch her fame and babble to their friends that they know her. The fairy dust of fame flickers through the air and all the people staring down at her stick their fingers on her sparkles and lick them ravenously.

If she ever gets out alive from this, she is going to do exactly what she likes, and it might not even be music. Maybe she isn't even meant to be a folkie.

She loves her fiddle. Tears start down her cheeks. She loves her violin. She will never play it again. She might die right here, and nobody will find her. Some coyotes or raccoons will come and eat her up. All that will be left will be her clothes. If a bear comes, he'll eat everything.

The snake feels heavy. Her head is spinning. She's still stoned. She's still drugged. What mean person was so insane to do this to her?

ADDICTED

Don leans back and shoves a pottery jar in front of him. He removes the top and peers into it with a fast-disappearing smile.

"Who took my pot?" he snorts.

"Don, you did. Last night, out on the deck. Made ten doobies and passed them around like wildfire," says Millie, who never misses a thing.

"No, I left some here for the morning." He looks around at the sleepy, red-eyed musicians.

"Coffee?" Millie asks.

"Sure!" the twins, Gordon and Jessie, say in unison.

Millie gestures over to the coffee pot and waves her hands at the long line of hanging mugs.

"Where are your parents?" Millie asks.

"Dunno," Gordon says.

"In the RV," Jessie says.

Gordon pours Jessie's and his coffee into the red and green mugs.

Just then, Martin pushes open the back door to the large kitchen. "Morning all," he says.

"Give us a tune," says Don, chuckling.

"Found the birthday girl?"

There is a silence while the twins look around.

"Must be upstairs," Gordon says, his blond, floppy hair covering one eye.

"Nope. She's still missing," Millie says, frowning.

"She'll turn up," Jessie says. "She always does."

"What do you mean, 'she always does'? Always when?" asks Millie.

"At parties in Berkeley," says Jessie. "You know. She goes off for a while with somebody, then reappears. Nobody much notices. Probably doing serious drugs in privacy behind a tree."

"She doesn't do serious drugs," protests Don, as he inhales deeply from a small joint and holds his breath.

"Not sure about that," Gordon says, finishing his coffee and pouring a second cup.

"What?" Millie says. "She's never done anything more than pot, and that's a fact."

There is a silence while all the musicians file through their cotton heads to see if they remember passing a joint to Beau.

"Yep," Gordon says. "She definitely smokes dope."

"But nothing more," proclaims Millie, daring the others to contradict her.

A lonely harmonica from the downstairs bedroom sounds something like a slow, sad Dylan. An accordion chimes in; then a mandolin and then a banjo and some guitars.

"They're addicted," Millie says, eyeing Don. "That's obvious. Can't even get a cup of coffee first. It's sick." She gazes at her banjo and wishes she could join them, too, and be addicted. Many more will be coming in for coffee in between licks, so she leaves her banjo alone.

Moonbeam and Misty shuffle in with their flip-flop sandals. Today, Moonbeam has fixed her hair in black braids. "Where's Beau?" she asks, aiming for the coffee pot.

Millie is grinding new coffee beans, and nobody feels like explaining the situation above the musical roar. Moonbeam looks around, then makes a face at Misty, who is flicking a fly off her fringed, tan jacket. Despite the music that continues from the other rooms, all their faces are too serious. This is the big annual jam. Why aren't they telling jokes? Why are they looking into their coffee cups?

"Where's Beau?" Moonbeam asks again. She looks at Misty, whose wide eyes beam with innocence.

Nobody Plays

Don is now pacing up and down the large kitchen. The long wooden table supports the half-asleep musicians staring into their mugs.

"Should we be worried?" he asks.

"Sit down, Don. You're making me nervous." Millie stands up and goes over to her distracted husband and puts her arm around his waist and guides him over to her vacant chair, steering him around and gently pushing him downwards. It isn't like she isn't going out of her mind, too, but it gives her something to do. Keeping calm under great stress isn't her best skill unless she meditates regularly, and she has not been doing that for years now.

The music blares louder and louder until Don's shock wave penetrates their song. "Stop playing!" he bellows, glancing at Millie. Everybody stops playing as if he is beckoning with the conductor's baton.

The silence is only disturbed by a badly propped up guitar cascading down the wall onto the kitchen floor and then the sound of the groans of sympathetic musicians. The leaves flutter ominously in the wind and a branch scrapes the stained-glass window above the exterior kitchen door.

"Nobody plays until we find Beau," Don announces sternly.

The collected group sits with their mouths open or covered with coffee cups.

Then chairs scrape away from the table almost in unison.

"Of course!" says Millie. "Let's find her so we can get on with the party—*her* party!" Millie says pointedly, annoyed at the ability of people there to ignore the strange absence of her daughter and be seemingly unconcerned.

Tiger's Touch

Beau yearns for Tiger's touch now, his soothing whisper in her ear, his way of holding her against his heart. She remembers their hurried coupling just that afternoon of her birthday — yesterday! Is it only the next day? She remembers an anxious feeling as she begged him to secretly lie with her: a feeling of foreboding, but with no idea why. And now she knows.

In her soul, Beau feels a need for Tiger's warmth and reassurance, with his long arms encircling her tiny frame. She has always felt so loved and taken care of by everyone. Then again, she remembers how there was that somber, lingering hesitation on her part yesterday when they went back from the barn to the Mansion to play music.

She sees them now: all her musical buddies with their mouths opened wide, singing *Happy Birthday to you,* and she remembers how she scanned their faces — a blur to her now. Was there one face that didn't quite express enough exuberance? All her girlfriends were there, swaying and blowing her kisses. The men bellowed as only that song can allow. *Perhaps someone wasn't wishing me a happy birthday: someone standing right in front of me — but who?*

DON AND MARTIN TAKE A BREAK

"I'm going out to smoke a bowl," Martin says.

"Want company?" asks Don, who's sworn off pot many times.

"Let's go," Martin says, fingering the small pipe in his pocket.

The two men walk over to the most secluded corner of the vast deck, sit down on the built-in wooden bench, and light up. In the bushes and trees in the near distance, the middle-aged musicians are looking for Beau while commenting and joking.

"Got to take a break from all this," Martin says, looking into the far distant pine trees down the mountain.

"It's killing me," Don confesses. "I've looked everywhere."

"She seemed perfectly fine when I played a duet with her around midnight," says Martin. "She was on fire! That girl can fiddle better than anybody I've ever heard."

Don chokes up and blames the pot smoke he's been holding in his lungs. "Yep," he says, coughing. "She's…" He coughs again and clears his throat, "…the best!"

"She wouldn't up and leave her own birthday party, would she, Don?"

"She has her moods…."

"Yeah! I've seen them through the years," Martin says.

"She can go into her room," says Don, "and sit curled up for hours. I don't know what she's thinking about. Sort of depressed or something."

"She wrote on Facebook that she thinks she has Asperger's."

"No way!" Don says, inhaling noisily as he opened up his lungs to an extra hard puff of pot, spluttering slowly, yet holding on, too. "Not in a million years!"

"Seriously. She put it on Facebook about six months ago: got hundreds of responses. Course, I never read them—I just skim it all—waste of time."

"Yeah," Don says. "I never look at that stuff. I'd rather do real music. I'm surprised she has time to mess around with it."

"She said it's imperative for her career."

"Look!" Don says, shifty and nervous, standing up and getting ready to start looking in some new place, like the other people. "She doesn't need that stuff. She's good. Everybody knows it. How can Facebook change that with a thousand 'likes'?"

"They say it helps!" says Martin, standing up, too.

"It's a new world," Don says. "I'd rather pull out my guitar and feel alive, not sit slumped in front of a darned computer!"

"They do it all on their phones now: even recordings," Martin says. "They don't slump. They do it walking, sitting on the john, after and before sex, in elevators, under dinner tables, while watching TV, and under the covers. It's sick!"

"Sounds compelling," Don says, sucking in one more hit.

"Compelling, is it?" Martin laughs, nodding at the disappearing joint in Don's fingers. "Well, guess we got to gear up and add our thoughts. Hey Don, I'm sorry about all this. We'll find her soon enough."

"We'd better. I'll personally strangle her if she's gone back to San Francisco. This party's costing us a small fortune!"

"We'll figure it out, Buddy. She's probably asleep nearby. After all, wasn't she playing only the night before to a huge crowd?"

"Yeah. She's just wiped out. But why wouldn't she sleep in her own room?"

They get up and saunter back into the house.

London:
Going to San Francisco

The young man waits for his parents to leave, for their chatter to fade out into the driveway and over to the car. As usual, his father is fussing and searching for his car keys. His mother wears her hat that she had to remove every time to get into the car. They sit back in their seats while the engine of their BMW warms up.

Of course, it is inconsiderate of him to disappear to a far-off country, just leaving his parents a cowardly note. But that is his plan. Years before, his disappointed parents had practically said goodbye to the genius they had so yearned for. His silence is only outward, but the turmoil of his soul inside never ceases.

The young man's suitcase is half-packed. He won't need heavy cardigans or coats in California. He tosses a few white, stiff-collared shirts on top out of habit, but his jeans, which he never wears in England, take top priority.

His whole persona is going to change. He has even practiced his American accent for a year. His passport is in his jacket pocket. His wallet is full of American dollars, plus a few pounds to get through Heathrow Airport and onto the plane. His violin is polished and ready in its case. He will buy a guitar there: steel-stringed this time, not nylon. His fingers itch to play folk music or jazz or something—just not classical! He feels wickedly like a chameleon and his colors are changing like a mirage as he admires himself in the big oblong mirror.

His parents will only be gone an hour. It is summer in both countries, so he will leave his large black umbrella and navy-blue overcoat at home. He checks his ticket, one way to San Francisco, British Air. At the last moment, he tosses one cardigan into his suitcase and then his new shaving bag and toothbrush. Looking around his room, he grabs a photo of his parents and himself when he was six, when they were still proud of him. He slips the fountain pen his father gave him into his bag of toiletries.

After one more look around his room, he reaches out and grabs a pile of classical violin music he knows so well by heart and slips it underneath all his packed clothes. His slippers beckon, but he leaves them behind. He looks back in the mirror, checks his teeth, puts on his jacket, straightening his tie. He can almost smell his freedom. His suitcase is quite heavy.

A sweep of bitter hatred falls over him as he turns, closes and locks the front door with a mean feeling of satisfaction, and flees down the stairway and out into the tall, black London taxi.

"Heathrow, please," he says, pushing his suitcase across the wide floor.

Through the loud crowds, all rushing in every direction, he boards the plane, pushing into the noisy, moving cocoon, and falls deeply into his novel. In ten hours and twenty minutes, he emerges with bleary eyes like a moth in a free land full of aging hippies.

The first thing he does is to make his way from the San Francisco International Airport to the St. Francis Hotel in Union Square. The very next thing he does is buy a cup of American coffee in a local bar, then purchase a new guitar. He clambers straight up into Union Square, takes out his brand new guitar, and starts playing and singing folk songs.

A crowd begins to gather. Applause and coins are not far behind!

THE SHERIFF

Rob, the sheriff and an old family friend, arrives at ten. Millie has known him over many years. He's been on the force a long time, and she's had him to tea and coffee and to some of her jams. He comes to her art exhibitions. They both like those landscapes dotted with old towns like the old gold mining town of Dutch Flat across the freeway.

As Rob enters the house, the musicians hold their coffee cups close to their chests. Rob was there the year before, so they know he plays bluegrass banjo in his spare time. Can't be all that bad: friendly guy, big smile and thick mustache; kind of like Gary Cooper in his manner. He's getting on, so he now gets the soft and easy jobs. His aching joints aren't visible, but you can't imagine him running after a thief, and he isn't the type to shoot first and ask questions later just to cover up his handicap. But the musicians see his full holster. What do they know? The older ones like Jim remember those Berkeley cops on Sproul Plaza beating up their friends all those years before: "blue meanies," they called them. A cop is a cop, no matter how gentle he appears.

A high note is plucked on somebody's guitar. You can't tell if it is an accident or a protest.

Millie pours a mug of coffee and walks over to him as he approaches the kitchen. The group makes a path for him, pulling in their boots or bare feet from the couches along the way.

"Mornin,' Millie," he says, with a calm familiarity.

"Glad you're here, Rob. Beau's still missing: we don't know where. She didn't say anything to anybody. Last seen by Tiger at 2 AM."

"Her truck's here, I noticed," Rob says.

"Yep: everybody's here who was here last night, so we need to figure this out. I'm sick with worrying. I know she's probably fine, but the party was for her — she turned eighteen — and it isn't like her to be so thoughtless as to leave without a grand farewell and a thank you." Millie rubs her left eye and blinks hard.

"Mornin,'" Rob says as he acknowledges the group gathering around him. "I guess I'd better have a look around myself and then I'd like to question everybody here."

"Whatever you need," Millie says. There is a mumbling noise of consent, and another string is plucked in the big room.

Rob downs his dregs and places the mug on the kitchen counter nearby.

"I know the place, so I'll go on through by myself. No need to bother you. Go on with your party. But I need more ideas from everybody."

Two musicians with long hair stuff their joints deep into their jeans' pockets and smile like children.

"I'll go with you, anyway," Millie says. "We can talk. Probably nothing to get excited about."

"They can go on playing," replies Rob. "No need to stop the party. We'll find out where she's gone soon enough."

"No," interjects Millie, frowning. "No music until she's found, and nobody leaves the house either, right Rob?"

Rob looks at Millie a long time, like he just realizes Millie isn't fooling. Perhaps Millie suspects foul play. Obviously, she feels something is truly amiss.

Just Disappeared

"Settle down, now," says Rob, once the group has come back into the living room: the rustling, rumbling, scraping chairs, muffled moaning and chuckles continue.

"Don't sit on my guitar!" yells somebody near the front.

"Sorry, buddy. I didn't mean to. Interesting guitar case you got there."

"All right! Any new information or any ideas?" Rob asks. The hush is stunning. Someone is chewing something, and it sounds like a dog.

Finally, at the back, Lee stands up, peering through her long bangs. "I think she's just disappeared. It's not like her. She always tells us where she's going to be. We're her friends! We would know. I think she's been kidnapped."

A groan and many sighs reverberate around the vast room. But nobody protests. Nobody contradicts her.

"Thank you," the sheriff says. "I see there's agreement on this subject. I'm afraid all of you are involved in this case. So, for now, you must stay here. I'll need a list of everyone who came and their addresses and phone numbers: that includes anybody living on this land. If you have neither, you still have to be on this list."

Some of the musicians keep mumbling on about music.

"But, I mean," says one musician in his fifties, "swing is different, like one, two and then that little pause, three, four, and a little pause."

"Well, I'm a blues man myself," says a nearby musician in his thirties, still half asleep.

Once in a while, Millie can be a patient woman, able to smile through adversity, and to hold her negative words back just a little longer, in case she is wrong. It has taken years of meditation, but it has worked. Coffee, however, can get in her way, and today she's had two cups, not her usual one. She scrapes back her chair with authority, and stands up, her back feeling slightly off-kilter. She puts her left hand on her hip and her right alongside her mouth, calling out to the mumbling, incoherent, sleepy, unshaven guitar heroes.

"Shut up!"

After a hushed pause, they go on finishing whispered ideas and theories, offering pot low down at hip level. You can't supply the whole bunch after all, but there is a subtle art of paying back for past favors that normally would have taken a small group out onto the deck.

Millie's attitude, normally so friendly, keeps them standing there. "This is not a political meeting, my friends," she says. "This is not a podium for theories. We need action. We need this property searched again, and that includes looking up in the trees as well as down at your shoes. I suggest a period of concentrated sobriety of all kinds if we are going to get this done. Let's get going. Be creative here, you slackers! Imagine a scenario and what might have happened. Go with your instinct."

"Can't we take one toke?" asks Jason. Everybody laughs nervously while some finger the plastic bags of pot in their pockets.

Tiger yells, "Shut up and get on with it!" The laughter subsides and everybody starts to leave the house. Don scrapes his chair back and stands up, and they all finally stop talking. He aims his beady eyes at each person in the crowd and nods his head. They scatter in all directions through the six doors out of the living area. Car doors and garage doors can be heard slamming. A couple of the locals who work part-time as woodchoppers, amble down the dirt road pointing up in the trees or over the mountainous horizon.

A billow of smoke wiggles its way from the distance and into the sky.

"Smoke! Fire!" yells Jake, hesitating at the front door, and pointing upwards.

"It's far away. Calm down," Jason says.

"Looks like the wind is blowing this way," says Jake.

"Keep your mind on our task, and let's find Beau. Sooner found, better music," says Don.

PATHS

Later on, Millie says to the crowd, who have come back empty-handed: "When she was a child, she used to take off down the mountain on paths we never knew about; shortcuts only children venture onto. Maybe she's on one of those paths? Has anybody checked them?"

"She took me down two of them, the steep one and the winding one," Tiger says.

"Did you look there?" Don asks, picking his teeth with his metal toothpick.

"I went down the winding one. I figured she wouldn't want to climb down the steep one at three in the morning."

"What if someone else was leading her down and didn't realize it was going to get steep?" suggests Millie, nibbling on what was left of the fingernails on her left hand.

"Well, if she went down the steep one with someone else, and if it was against her will, it would be someone who lives on the land here," Millie says. "Let's gather all the rest of the gang in here and ask them and see what they might know."

"I reckon a few have gone back to their vans and cabins by now," Tiger says.

"I told everybody to search and then come back to the house until she's found. Bring them back in here right now!" grumbles Don, who is fishing for another cigarette. Millie frowns at him, so he puts his hands back on his mug and grunts.

"I'll get them," Tiger says, pushing past a few lingering young women who think they can sing like angels, their arms wrapping around each other's shoulders, their bright red lips dangling rings, their hair dyed black.

"All right, you guys," he says to the men eyeing the girls, "toss your roaches and get into the kitchen."

"We ain't done nothin,'" Screwball moans.

"Ya gotta come anyway. We need ideas."

At that, Screwball sits up. "Come on, you lazy SOBs. Git in there and confess!"

"Fuck you," Scrawny says, his greying beard halfway down his chest.

"Get up!" Tiger commands.

"Oh, fuck it!" Scrawny answers, flipping his cigarette butt into the ashtray and missing.

"Hey, put it out," says Tiger. "There's already one fire down the mountain. Don't need one here."

Scrawny reaches over and daintily picks up the smoky stuff and smashes it to flakes, smiling at Tiger.

After a while, a scraggly group of dusty-hatted men of all ages who live on the land shuffle back through the living room and into the kitchen.

"Sit down, fellas," Millie says.

Chairs are scraped out and they all sit down like they would rather be anywhere else.

"Who knows where the steep path is?" asks Don.

"We all do," Scrawny bellows.

"Okay! Every one of you get back out there now and search the bushes near the path," says Rob.

A sigh of relief goes through the room. The men shuffle out of the kitchen like they are wearing slippers, not cowboy boots.

"All right," yells Tiger, "The rest of you people, let's really check this Mansion and find out where's she's crashed! Let's go!"

Upon this command, everybody else swallows the last gulps of their Diet Cokes and iced coffee cups, scraping back their chairs in unison.

"You go back upstairs," Tiger says to the younger bunch. "And leave your instruments here!"

There are disgruntled and startled looks and groans.

"I mean it! No jamming until she's found!"

"You old folks, you shining bunch of hot players," says Tiger. "You get this floor — look everywhere, all closets, bathrooms, behind couches. I mean, this time really look! Think! Be creative!"

A look of relief passes over the white-haired bunch. Notes are accidentally plucked on all the instruments as if in final protest. Another guitar, leaning precariously up against the kitchen cabinet, slowly timbers onto the flagstone floor, creating a loud communal groan.

"You," Tiger commands to the ones in their thirties and forties. "Outside: old outhouses, trailers, vans, tree houses; anywhere. Listen. Your job is to find her. Maybe she's there but can't talk. Maybe she's…never mind."

Everybody knows where his thought has gone and most looked pained and busy with their chairs and guitars.

After over an hour of searching, almost everybody, sweltering hot, wanders back into the house and sits down in the kitchen, drinking cold water and Cokes, or in the living room, flopping down on the couches.

SUSTENANCE

"Let's face it," says Millie, "she's really disappeared. It's not like her to disappear. She always tells me if she's off down the road." Millie's mouth is turned down at the corners. Misty steps forward and puts her arm around Millie's shoulders.

The other men who are still outside straggle back into the house, blowing one last puff of their cigarette or pot smoke outside the doors. One by one, they step in, brushing their boots and sandals, looking like they'd lost something, looking like they were loath to tell Millie that they've failed in their mission.

The sheriff beckons them towards the kitchen. Don is tossing handfuls of cut up potatoes into the largest iron frying pan a person could lift. He stirs vigorously, then starts whisking three-dozen eggs and a quart of milk into a huge cooking bowl.

"A man can't blunder through these tick-infested bushes without sustenance," he says. "Coffee'll only get you so far." Don glances at Millie who is reaching for six long loaves of French bread. The loaves all tumble onto the floor. It is as if she's lost her sight, like she is feeling her way towards them, but isn't seeing anything directly in front of her. She bends down to retrieve them and Tiger steps over and crouches down, gathering them all up in his muscular arms at once, and places them back on the counter.

"Thanks, Tiger. Can you help me open...?"

"'Course I can. You go sit down and have more coffee. I got the toast." He wipes something from his eye and hustles like a young man eager to have something to do.

"Butter's in the refrigerator," Don says to Frisky, the guy from San Francisco. Frisky scoots over to the refrigerator and hauls out large cakes of restaurant-sized butter and starts unwrapping it, standing next to Tiger.

"Nothing?" he says quietly to Tiger.

"Not a hint. Not a fucking thing. Fuck!"

Tiger throws down the butter knife and stands ominously still. "Where the fuck did she go?"

Everyone in the kitchen stops and looks at Tiger. It is as if he has become immobile for fear of his own rage.

Rob steps across the kitchen. "Tiger, buddy, she's here some-where. Or back in the Bay Area. We'll find her. But time is our enemy here. Eat up, you all, and fast. We've got to keep this search going all day. There's a fire out there, far enough away, according to my iPad, but not contained. If it gets a lot closer, we'll have to evacuate."

"I'm not evacuating," blurts Tiger. "I've got a gas mask in my trunk. I'm not leaving until I find her." He shoves a loaf of bread to-wards Rob. "Here, you toast it. I'm outta here." The sheriff follows him outside.

At this point, the fries smell divine; the scrambled eggs are gooey, but not runny. The toast is popping out of the toaster and the butter is melting. The huge Costco strawberry jam jars are opened with a knife handle standing up in each of them. As Tiger stomps away, Mil-lie gets up and begins serving generous servings onto the paper plates. They will go back out, but after three hours, the rest of them feel a good breakfast is their due, especially as not one more note is going to be allowed to be played or sung!

"Are you assuming she's dead?" Don asks.

"Of course not!" George replies.

"She's not dead," Millie says, brushing the crumbs off the edge of the table and pouting. "Maybe she's fallen in the dark and hit her head or sprained her ankle!"

"Maybe she had a fight with Tiger and he's not letting on!" Art says.

"They don't fight. They just ignore each other," Ted says.

"So, there it is. She's walked down the mountain and is spending time at the local gas station. Serves him right!" Don says.

"Where's her fiddle?" Millie asks the ceiling.

"It's in the living room," Don says.

"Oh, yes, I forgot!" mumbles Millie.

"She's probably hitched to San Francisco and is playing on the streets for her supper," George says.

The sheriff's voice can be heard outside giving orders. It gets louder as they all trudge up the few wide wooden stairs surrounding the deck.

"Not without her fiddle!" Millie says, eyeing George.

QUESTIONED

One by one, they come back yet again, dusty and exhausted. Martin reaches out to Millie, and they embrace gently. Don comes over and opens his arms wide and Martin and Millie gather him in for a group hug. Tiger opens his arms and is pulled in for a swaying, quiet and open-ended moment of solace. They begin to rock and sway. Rob doesn't join in, however. He has never broached that familiarity while on duty and he won't — even now.

"Martin and I have searched all the vans and the cabins," he says, breaking the swaying hugging moment into manageable parts. They slowly open the circle and slide their hands off each other's shoulders.

"Sit down," Millie offers, her hand indicating the stuffed chair and the long couches. They all sit down like obedient school children, waiting for Rob's comments.

"Well?" Millie coaches.

"Nothing, sorry," he says. "Or not. We can still hope she's on the road."

There are murmurs of agreement.

"Tiger?" Rob continues. Tiger looks up and raises his eyebrows. "You're sure you didn't have a fight with Beau last night?"

"Of course, I'm sure. She made a comment about hating my smoke and the awful taste of my kisses, but she always says that."

"So quit!" Don says, fingering his cigarettes.

"Thinking about it," Tiger says.

"Quit!" Millie adds.

"Look," Rob interjects, "This is serious. It's not about Tiger's smoking. It's about their relationship last night."

"End of story, then," says Tiger. "It's perfect and always was."

"Okay. Leave it," Rob says.

"What now?" Tiger asks.

"All the tents, vans and cabins have been searched," Rob says. "I'm at a loss. Any ideas?"

"Call the police!" Martin jokes, smiling at Rob.

Everybody snickers.

"First of all," Rob says, seriously eyeing the crowd. "We have no evidence that there is foul play; just a suspicion that her behavior has been unexpected and unusual: especially on her big eighteenth birthday. She knew that you two went through a lot to put this party on. I know she loves you, so we have to assume she wouldn't act like a spoiled brat and just leave in a temper."

"She has a temper," Martin mumbles.

"True," Don says.

"Not often," Millie says.

"Often enough," Tiger says, fingering his own cigarettes in his pocket.

The group looks at one another blankly.

"Should we just wait it out?" asks Don.

"Not my style!" Rob says, wiping his sweaty brow. "Back outside! Go further uphill, and some of you check lower down the road. Go as far as the freeway."

SMOKE

Somehow the smallest sliver of air flows through a tiny break in the tape covering Beau's mouth. It surprises her. After all, she has, without a thought, gulped in air all her life. Now, with one more exhausting push of her tongue while her diaphragm fights for breath, a minuscule gap in the tape allows the tiniest amount of air into her lungs and she realizes, as she pulls the air down her throat, just how important any air at all is to her continued survival.

Beau tries to wiggle her bound feet. Her bare legs are cold and numb. Her fingers pull and pick at the tight binding around her wrists. She has a strange longing to suck her thumb.

Suddenly she feels a scratchy feeling near her ankle. Then she hears a slight breathing sound. Both of her legs are being touched by something light, like whiskers. A tongue licks her ankle. She feels teeth around her big right toe, brushing against her sandals.

She can't move. She longs to kick and scream, but just the effort of pulling in that precious breath of air is all she can do to survive. She can't help it! She instinctively kicks the creature hard. A smell she hates filters into her nostrils. Teeth are gentle on her toe. There comes a sucking feeling like the animal has found its mother. It stops and Beau feels it turn against her leg, rubbing its fur against her foot. Then she can hear the quiet pat of paws retreating. The sharp smell of the animal makes her realize it is a skunk, maybe a baby skunk. Just as she realizes it in relief, the departing skunk's lingering smell chokes her. She is forced to breathe in this powerful smell and be grateful for the air at the same time.

In the silence, she hears and feels the rapid beating of her heart now subsiding. She pushes the tape with her tongue, again and again, and feels the gap opening a little more. Somehow, even the awful thought of the skunk returning gives her more energy to try to break free. And the snake still rests on her neck.

Then she smells smoke: just a whiff. It isn't cigarette smoke or pot smoke. She starts wiggling and moving and tearing at her wrists and pushing at the tape all at the same time. Nobody knows where she is. They will all leave her alone to die of asphyxiation and burns even if that kidnapper never returns. She dares not cry: her dry mouth hungers for moisture. The smell of smoke becomes more alarming.

I won't cry. I won't cry!

A Band Without a Name

Millie goes over her list. Some people are above suspicion. She stops on Moonbeam's name. What kind of dippy parents would put that name onto a baby? Well, now that Millie remembers, Moonbeam's part Native American parents wear all the hippie garments right into the present day: that leather coat her father Michael wears with the Native American fringe, covered in Peace buttons, and his guitar case covered in Peace sayings. He wears moccasins right through winter and he has a Native American pot pipe, complete with turquoise beading.

Turns out, Moonbeam loves her name. A lot of kids changed back to Nancy and Susan and Mary just to be like their other friends. Not Moonbeam: she likes being different. She wore her hair in braids until she was eighteen and then shaved her head bald. Then, for a while, she had a cute, short-cropped style with one long wisp on the back of her neck, slightly to the left side. She wears her newly growing long hair in a dark, thick braid down her back, as often as not, entwined with Indian beads.

Young Moonbeam had played the clarinet, driving everybody crazy with her first attempts at jamming. But over the years, she has turned out to be an accomplished musician. She and Beau play together all the time, bouncing off each other's riffs, making up odd phases that turn into jazzy melodies, and casting an awed silence among the other jammers as they zip along up and down the scales, like a game between friends. Applause is never far behind.

Sometimes Tiger has to pry the two young women apart to get any time with Beau. He wishes Moonbeam would get back together with David, the beer-drinking harmonica player. The four of them play so often they are taken as a band without a name. But they enjoy floating around, too, and finding out more about themselves as musicians when joining an older group.

Millie looks around the kitchen, then over the heads of the group and realizes that Moonbeam isn't around. Maybe she and Beau went on a moonlight walk and got lost?

"Where's Moonbeam?" Millie asks. People look around as if expecting her to be standing right behind them.

"Who saw her last?" asks Don, aiming his face at David.

"Not me!" David splutters.

"She was playing over by the fireplace most of the night with those old guys. Can you believe that, with her talent! Sorry buddy!" he adds to his old friend, Sam, the white-bearded washboard player sitting right next to him.

"Hey!" Moonbeam complains, as Jordon pulls her into the kitchen from around a corner.

"So," Millie asks, her hands on her hips. "Where have you been?"

Moonbeam smiles sheepishly. "Been with our group."

"There're all in here," responds Millie.

"Yeah, well—before. I just took a shower," she says.

Millie squints at Moonbeam's wet hair and realizes she now suspects everyone there. She desperately needs a nap.

DESPERATION AND SHAME

Just the week before Beau's party, a facet of a long-forgotten memory surfaces. The kidnapper hardly catches it, right in the middle of the most complicated stretch of his solo, surrounded by a bass guitar player, two banjo players, a mandolin player, and a harmonica player.

In his memory of five years before, he sees Beau in another group across the large room, head bowed, her fingers a blur, perhaps like his own, up and down the fingerboard. At thirteen, her fiddle notes filter faintly in between his own and he remembers his own childhood with his lean fingers almost like a clock speeded up, pushing on like a sturdy machine, not one note missed, not one pitch out of tune, and yet some subtle feeling added to the music that only a brilliant musician can express. He remembers the Professor's face, his stern glare that pushed excellence into his young fingers while his parents nodded in approval.

He remembers feeling like a robot on show, how a slight pat on his cheek would be his only reward. Yet so desperate is he for even that moment that his musical efforts become perfection. But only if he performs in front of an audience will it gain him a brief hug from his mother. When had she stopped hugging him? Was he three? And he can't even remember when his father did anything more than a congratulatory handshake and an English nod of approval. He sees other parents giving those brief hugs. He wishes for a brother to tumble and play with along with that tactile reward. Even a dog would help.

"No animals in our house!" says his stern father.

The child stands at attention, exhausted from continually trying to be perfect, and says, "Good afternoon, Father," and dashes upstairs past the portraits of his ancestors, into his large Victorian bedroom and onto his one place of solace: his eiderdown and soft duck-feathered pillows. But he doesn't cry. Again, his stomach squeezes violently and so he has to rise up, tear down the hall to the brown-colored seat in the *w.c.*, and sit down in desperation and shame.

PEOPLE TAKE PATHS

"Check out that smoke," Don says to the exhausted musicians.

People start sniffing like their caveman forebears. In unison, they get up and walk out to the deck and around the corner to the narrower side of the deck. In the distance, the dark cloud is growing larger.

"Not good," murmurs Don.

"Winds blowing this way," David says.

"I can see red lights," Tiger says. "Fire trucks."

"That's good," David says.

"And bad," adds Don. "It's burning so much nearer to the house!"

They watch awhile, then turn like a school of fish and swarm back into the house. People shuffle and sit in the giant living room in small groups, some at the large, round wooden table, some on the extra-long leather couches, some in the broken circles of chairs left over from the night before. Some stand by the door as if news will stream through and tell them what to do.

"Might have to evacuate," suggests Millie, dragging her fingers across her banjo, still propped up on its stand. People look up, almost ready to seize their instruments for a short break, if only to be normal for a moment, like there is no fire and no missing Beau.

"This is urgent!" says Rob. "We have to get out again and search! This time, go a different way. You might notice something staring you right in the face that your guitar-picking friends walked right by."

"Let's go!" Tiger says, leaping up from a straight-backed chair and tapping the twins on their backs.

Rob walks out to his car, its light still blinking on and off. He picks up his phone and leans inside to check his laptop.

"Fire's twenty per cent contained," he announces as the women and men file around his car, which seems to be importantly blocking some of their vehicles.

People throw glances towards the smoke.

Millie says, "Go towards the smoke. If she's out there, we want to get to her first!"

They spread out and begin to climb down the mountain. It is eerily quiet apart from the coughing of the smokers. The women with good shoes get down the mountain with flair. The ones who have only brought flip-flops keep to the road.

"P.U.!" shouts Alisha.

"Skunk!" Moonbeam says.

Their small group comes to a standstill while a small skunk waddles away down the road and dips into the bushes.

"I'm not going that way!" Moonbeam is holding her nose. She turns back up the hill. The rest follow.

Alisha says, "Here's a path. Let's try it."

"That's where the baby skunk was. Maybe there are more babies following her at a safe distance, and then the mother," decides Moonbeam.

"Don't be paranoid—it's a path," says Alisha. "People take paths. Maybe Beau took that path last night."

"Maybe not. She's probably back in San Francisco laughing her head off," says Moonbeam.

"I'm taking it!" Alisha says. "Coming?"

They all turn and follow Alisha away from Beau.

"Hey!" says Alisha, bending down and picking up a piece of cloth. "What's this?"

The group stared at it. It isn't old and dirty. It is a torn piece of a pocket, perhaps from shorts, with a hint of blue and black.

"What was Beau wearing last night?" asks Alicia.

"Her blue shorts?" suggests Misty.

It has been a hot evening. Beau could have been wearing shorts. She came back into the party so late. It isn't what any of the musicians care about at that time. The music is all that matters at eleven o'clock at night.

"Mmmmmm," Beau mumbles, but the voices of her friends disappear into the distance.

The snake wiggles. Beau can hardly breathe.

BEAU'S SHORTS

The sun is growing hotter. The morning hours drift into short shadows. In the distance, the smoke cloud grows larger. Helicopters dump billows of orange onto the dancing red sparkle.

"Looked everywhere," Tiger says, his eyebrows creased, his guitar long stowed. "Nothing!"

"It's going to be a hot one," Don says. "If she's out there, she might be dehydrated, parched!"

"It'll be a bloody site hotter if they don't put that fire out soon," Geoffrey says.

"They're on it," Millie states with a fragile quiver in her voice.

"Still spreading," Rob reminds them. "We really might have to think about getting out of here. Gather your photographs," he nods at Millie.

"Paintings and photos," she corrects, and jumps up. "But first we have to find Beau."

"If we can't find her, we'll still have to leave. After all, she could be in the Bay area, as you've mentioned," says Rob.

"I'm not leaving. Don, load up my best paintings into the truck. And be careful. But I'm staying here."

"Her cell's here," Tiger reminds her.

"She's been known to borrow a stranger's cell phone when her battery dies, which is frequently," says Millie.

"Maybe that's why her phone is here—dead battery." Tiger suggests.

"Nope. It still works. Let's keep it plugged in," says Rob, hunting through the phone for clues. "Tiger, do you know her phone's code?"

"Try 4621. Last video opened is of her winning that fiddle contest in Colorado. That was two months ago. But I saw her check it yesterday."

"Let's look at it again," Rob says. He picks up the phone from the table, turns it on and taps in the code.

In a flash, the YouTube video is playing. "I took that very video and put it on YouTube."

"Okay," Rob says. "That person standing nearby looks suspicious. Everybody else is tapping their feet. This man behind her is almost like a statue."

"Let me see that," Tiger says, grabbing the phone and tapping a few buttons. "Oh, that's Ralph. He has depression problems. Probably overdosed on his pills. He looks way out of it," he adds, leaning down and showing Don, then Millie.

"He's here, isn't he?" Millie wonders aloud.

"Yep. Think he might have gone out with Ted for a smoke," Tiger says.

"Maybe he has some insight into why Beau looked at this video again after she'd seen it a dozen times."

"She always does that," says Tiger.

"Shall we wait or go get them?" said Don, who often preferred instructions to using his own initiative.

"Which way did they go?" Millie asks.

"They probably went down the driveway. Too chicken to take the overgrown dirt paths," Tiger says, putting the phone back on the table, leaving it plugged in.

"Go out and yell down that driveway. Get them back up here," the sheriff commands. "I want to know what's going on here with this video. Maybe nothing. Maybe something, though."

A few musicians drift back into the house, hunting for cold drinks.

"Beer can wait," says the sheriff, picking up the phone from the table again, and then putting it back down. "Stick to soft drinks and water until we find her."

"Shit!" One young man and one old guy snort into their chests.

"No luck," George says, reaching into the huge ice chest for bottled water that the saw player, Morgan, always brings.

The voices of young women arriving filter into the living room and all heads turn their way as Alicia holds out a small, fragile piece of torn cloth.

"This comes from Beau's shorts," she announces triumphantly, her forehead dripping.

"Oh, hell!" Millie says. "That means she's here somewhere!"

Alicia shuffles and looks down, then up. "I am pretty sure she was wearing blue shorts."

AGONY

"Stand up straight!" Professor Klimpt says, his eyebrows frowning over his glaring eyes. He stands so tall that the growing boy thinks his own head will disengage and roll onto the Turkish rug. Now the Professor leans down into the boy's frame, like the boy's presence makes the Professor's back ache, and worse. His large face comes close until the cigar breath shocks the boy such that he blinks as his eyes water.

"Perfect!" says the Professor. "You are ready to perform!" But the sixteen-year-old boy, who has grown inches in the past two years, lays his instrument in its case and dashes to the toilet with a string of apologies and the yowl of tears when he doesn't quite make it in time.

One day, a year later, as he sits waiting for his parents to conclude some kind of conference with Professor Klimpt, he can see the same disappointed faces from his fur-clad mother and his hat-holding father.

"You are a failure," says his father after the Professor leaves. Standing near the grand piano, he hits the back of the teenager's head again, pushing him forward so that he trips and falls down.

"Get up, you lazy boy!" says his disappointed father. The teenager struggles up, all the while holding the back of his head to fend off more blows.

"You will go into your room!" says his mother. "And no supper!" she adds.

The boy carries his bow and his larger violin, which had been given to him the year before by his hopeful father, upstairs to his room and lays them down on the bed.

"This was played by your grandfather," his father had told him. Maybe it will be taken away like his little violins had disappeared. Maybe he is so bad they won't ever let him play again. And yet, he feels alive and powerful playing those notes on the violin that he imagines in his head.

When he practices alone at home, he hardly ever has to dash to the toilet. But after he plays for his professor and his parents, the rumblings begin in his stomach, and he must leave for the toilet the moment he is finished playing. The bewildered looks of his mother are hard to endure.

He doesn't know why he has that reaction. He tries not to run off. He tries so very hard! But it is no use. His mother's look of ecstasy after he plays turns to agony as he speeds by her face, which he can just see in a teary blur, falling from a satisfied smile into a searing frown.

Rattlesnake!

Not long after the girls leave, it bothers Beau that the skunk is still nibbling on her big toe. Thankfully, it wobbles off without taking it with him. But the snake on her neck has almost stopped her breathing. If she breathes, will it bite her? If her heart races, will it rattle its tail in her ear and sink its teeth into her jugular? So far, it seems content now just lying over her throat and enjoying the coolness of the shelter.

Muffled voices filter into her ears. At last! A search party! She hears someone say, "Beau..." How difficult to focus on faraway chatter when all her energy is concentrated on her sleeping companion. Yet, there it is: voices coming closer. And closer.

"What's this?" she hears Tiger say. *What is what? What does he see? Did he find my cell phone? No, I don't have it with me.*

"Nothing," says Geoffrey. "Toss it away."

"Nope. It's going in my pocket. All evidence, no matter how...."

Oh, Tiger, keep walking! I'm just below your voices? I can't speak! I can't move. This snake will kill me.

The voices stop. She wiggles. A soft, steady rattling sound near her ear stiffens her whole body. This is it. She can't move her mouth. Her throat is dry and stuck closed. One sound could possibly finish her off. She lies there, her heart racing with this awful contradiction. The girls didn't hear her last time.

Beau remembers how she has always liked to take risks. She remembers how she threw herself off those high diving boards. She remembers standing with her fiddle poised in front of a huge audience in Golden Gate Park, how her knees shook so much she almost collapsed, and yet, the bow began to dance all on its own, the knocking in her knees disappeared, and then her head and body were alive with her joy in the expression she somehow created that made people laugh and dance and sing. Her mind reaches into that space. Her fiddle is poised, the bow is raised; her left elbow presses near her ribs; her eyes gaze at her left hand, then her lids close and she is there, beyond fear, beyond a snake and its rattle. She gently allows the air into her mouth. The rattling becomes fiercer. Beau starts to say, "Hmmmm."

"Listen!" Tiger says. "A rattlesnake! Let's get out of here!"

In reaction to his voice, the snake practically leaps off her neck and lands on her legs. A horrible skunk smell still fills her nostrils. Is that a dying sound? Is it faltering by her toes?

Beau hears the voices fading, the feet scuttling away. Even if she can make another sound now, will they hear it in their fright?

"Hmmmm," she tries.

What is that furry thing tickling her leg? She gags on the smell. She feels the snake slither across her shins and then it seems to be gone. She imagines its swift departure, away from the smell. Again, she begins pushing the tape with her tongue with what little saliva she can produce and is afraid to think why there is a helicopter flying above her and, if there is, in fact, a forest fire.

LEAVING

The snake is gone, but the skunk smell battles with the smoke smell. If someone walks by again, Beau might be able to make a noise. It is warming up now. Daylight filters through her covered eyelids. She sniffs. The smell of smoke becomes stronger. No footsteps can be heard. The smoke is lingering. It doesn't smell like a cigarette, but rather a pine tree. Beau hears voices in the distance. She hears cars and trucks and motorcycles starting their engines. This means one thing: it isn't someone burning the brush deliberately, but rather people evacuating the ranch. She tries to wiggle out but makes no progress. She mumbles but knows no one can hear her above the increasing rattling of the cars and vans passing so close to her down the road. The smoke is getting stronger. Now she has even more difficulty breathing. She chokes. Surely Rob will find her. She cocks her ears.

Beau remembers how her mom taught her to meditate and starts in again with her long-lost mantra. At least she has something else to do with her mind besides worry about her impending rape and death. *But why has he left me here?*

Om, she says to her brain. *When is he coming back? Om,* she pushes it into her brain with a firm kick. *Why does he want to do this to me? Om, a thousand, om, a thousand, om, a thousand, om.*

Om! Om! Om! She presses on, chasing her thoughts away with her mental armor.

Mom! I'm here. I'm next to a skunk and a snake! Smell the skunk, Mom. Don't leave me here! The skunk! She gags as focusing on the smell now blasts her brain. She brings it into her mind and sends it out to Millie. Cars and vans are rolling a hundred yards from her down the gravely dirt driveway. Smoke blends with that skunk smell. No! Not smoke. *It's the skunk, Mom, the skunk smell! Mom, I'm here! Don't leave me! Please, please, don't leave me here!*

More musicians are in the driveway now and start coughing: one, then two, and then everybody. Martin and Tiger are especially agitated, glancing around furtively while the others lug their crumpled tents and guitar cases across the large driveway turnaround and into their vehicles.

"I think we need to leave now. Everybody else is in their cars," Don shouts, checking the smoke high in the sky and down the mountain.

"I'll stay until last," Rob says, turning and shouting at the cars. "Go to the Auburn Hospital to hang out while we decide what they should do. Stay in the parking lot. You are still all under investigation. But you must go, now!"

"I'm staying," Millie shouts.

"Me, too," Don says.

"Get moving," Rob shouts, checking his laptop once again, his car lights flashing. "The fire is out of control. It's heading this way."

"I'll stay and make sure everybody's left," Martin says.

"I'll stay, too," Tiger says.

"No," shouts Rob. "You two have to make sure these people all get to the hospital safely. Consider yourselves my deputies from now on."

"I can still be your deputy and stay here!" Tiger protests. "Maybe Beau is hiding and the smoke will make her surface!"

"You go," Martin says. "I'll stay behind with Millie and Don."

"Martin; Tiger: orders—get out of here! Now!" Rob commands.

"Where's Ralph?" Martin mumbles.

"Haven't seen him since last night," Tiger says.

"Has anybody seen him?" Rob says. Nobody answers. "Now, get going!"

Martin and Tiger scurry over to their vehicles. "Let's go," Martin says, leaping into his truck.

"Alright. I'll drive Beau's truck," Tiger says, picking up the keys on her truck's front seat floor, and turning on the engine.

"I'll drive yours," says Geoffrey.

"You're a pal," says Tiger, tossing him his car keys.

"Everybody, go, go, *go!*" Rob shouts.

Old trucks and newer cars are following each other, rumbling down the driveway, bumping hard over ruts in the driveway, alarming animals that are still holding out, and prompting complaining jays to join in the general cacophony.

The cars and trucks disappear into the distance of fading sound down the mountain.

Around the corner, Martin screeches back up the driveway in his truck.

"I am not leaving without Beau!" he yells to Rob.

79

Not Leaving

"No!" yells Millie. "I'm not leaving either 'til we've found her," she shouts at Don. "Let go of me!"

"We have to go now!" yells Don.

"I will not leave this place until we find her. I'd rather be burned alive," yells Millie.

Mom! I'm here! Beau closes her eyes and concentrates so hard she almost forgets to breathe. *Om! Om! Om!*

"I know she's here!" yells Millie.

"We've got to go!" yells Don.

"You have to come NOW!" commands the sheriff.

Mom, Mom! Don't go! Don't leave me here! I'm by the skunk, by the smell.

Millie breaks away from their grasp and runs down the driveway, sniffing into the air. "I'm staying, that's final! Let go of me! Stop! I know she's here! I know it! I can smell it. The skunk. The skunk. Follow that smell! Here! She's here somewhere. Very nearby!"

Don and Rob hunker after Millie, grab her arms, and drag her as she screams in protest up the driveway and back to the sheriff's car.

"Millie, you are temporarily under arrest! It is my duty to save you!"

"It's my duty to save my daughter!" Millie screams as she shifts from one side of the car to the other side of the seat and leaps out of the opposite door and runs past the car and back down the driveway.

"Drive it down," Don commands, as he runs down after Millie. "I'll get her."

Mom! Come here! "Mmmmmmm."

"She's here somewhere—p.u! Near that skunk smell. I feel it, Don!"

Don steps next to her and sniffs. "Horrible! Are you positive, Millie!"

"I know it for sure!"

Martin leaves his truck idling and follows Don and Millie down the path. Don bumps into her as Millie comes to an abrupt halt.

"Get in the car!" yells Rob. "It's too late! Martin! Get the hell out of here!"

All of them are coughing.

Beau chokes on a cough.

"Stop! Don't move!" says Millie.

Martin hears a cough and points. "Over there!"

Beau gets out another muffled, short cough.

"Did you hear it?" Millie shouts. "There! There!"

They charge down through the bushes and towards the shallow hole and Don gets down and crawls towards it.

"Oh, my God! She's here!" he yells.

"Beau!" yells Millie.

"Get her out! Let's get out of here!" shouts Rob.

They all pull Beau out by the feet. The snake is nowhere in sight.

"Calm down, now, Beau, hold on!" Millie says, as she peels the duct tape from around Beau's head and from her mouth and then unties her feet.

Beau inhales with a dry, wheezing squeal, and gulps in two full breaths before she screams like a bursting cloud!

"Calm down, Mom? Fuck that bastard!" she yells, scraping at her hair.

Beau tries to stand up but falls down. "The snake is gone! Oh, my God!"

Millie put her arms around her, helps her stand up, and Don pulls her hands towards him. Beau throws her arms around Don, and weeps with an open mouth, like she is retrieving her ability to fully breathe. Martin gives her a brief hug, then runs back to his truck, jumps in and takes off down the mountain, nodding to Rob. "I'll catch up with the others," he yells. "Love you, Beau!"

The sheriff draws nearer. "We have to go right now! Thank God you're alive!" He grabs Beau and ferries her, limping, to his car.

NOT THAT SMELL

The three of them push back up the path to the dirt and gravel driveway and the sheriff tells Beau to sit in the back behind him. Don gets in front and Millie climbs into the other side and puts her arm around Beau. The doors slam with a finality that is not really there. They slam with anger, relief, a warning: unfinished business. They slam loud and hard, as if to say, there will be another day and we will find you, you bastard!

"That smell! Horrible, horrible!"

"We'll be away from it soon," Rob says, dodging the potholes in the curving road.

"No, no! Not that smell. Another smell! What is that smell! I hate it! Yuck! It's horrible! I have to get out! I have to get away!" Her hand grasps the door handle, but Millie snaps her safety belt off and grabs Beau's hand. Beau is choking. She starts retching. She pushes the button to open the window. It won't open.

"Open the windows!" Beau yells and thumps the sheriff's shoulder. He buzzes her window open, and she lunges her head out, pulling the forest air into her lungs like a drowning swimmer.

"I can't stop now," shouts the sheriff. "The fire is sweeping up the mountain. We'll be lucky to get out of here if we step on it hard." He pushes the gas pedal and the car tears around a curve, bumping over the potholes and swerving around a leaping deer and her two babies.

Millie says, "What was that?" as a huge buck lands on the other side of their car. Confused birds squawk. A mountain of animals seems to be charging uphill and away from the encroaching fire and smoke. It is as if the whole side of it were alive.

"Run!" yells Beau through the window. "Run away!"

Come and Get Me

Ralph, flat on his back, is waking up and can only see blue sky. He wonders if anybody will even find him in time. He can't move his left arm and his face feels strange. With his right hand, he touches his cheeks and his lips. He tries to say, "Help!" but nothing comes out. His throat seems stuck together and his lips feel like they overlap his chin. He blinks without a problem, but the rest of his head feels dead. He sees the tall pine trees above him and the bright morning sky between the branches. He can hardly breathe and sucks in the cold air and pushes it out. He hears the strain on his lungs from the inside of his head and feels a desire to move back towards the road, but his body won't respond to his short-circuited commands.

Why did he veer off the road in the early hours when he heard a car coming? If he had stayed on it and waved like they do in the country, somebody could have found him. He realizes it is because he has had a stroke. What else can this be? He grasps the prickly dry grass and tries to pull his heavy body along. Perhaps he is an inch closer to the road, but he is immobilized and exhausted.

He coughs silently. How will he be able to play the fiddle ever again in this condition? He is going to be burned alive. Now he will be wiped off the scene and probably be forgotten all too soon.

Nobody will remember him: too unshaven, too many holes in his sneakers; too yellow a smoker's lip, stubby orange and cracked fingers.

Ralph slaps his cheeks and lifts his bottom lip. He feels nothing. His lip goes back near his chin. His mouth remained open. A squirrel above him leaps from tree to tree. He must have been there a good five hours.

He hears voices. They are so nearby. He hears the giggles and the screams of, "P.U.! A skunk!" He thumps the ground with his fist, but they are now disappearing into the distance, and the giggling is fading away. A tear swims down the side of his head. He coughs, but no sound comes out. Then vans and trucks rumble by him. The sheriff is commanding Millie to get back into the car.

No! Come and get me! I'm right here! Ralph shouts silently.

The skunk walks right by him. Ralph feels like vomiting.

THE JACKET

It smells like that man. Beau retches again, even as she gulps in the smoky pine air from the window. That horrible man smelled like chloroform!

"What's going on, Beau? Can we help you?" asks Millie.

"Mom, it's that smell. It smells like chloroform. That man smelled like chloroform!" She gags.

"Yes," Millie says. "I can smell it, too. Where's it coming from?" Millie sniffs and looks around the inside of the police car. She reaches down to the leather coat lying behind the sheriff's seat, pulling it up to her nose, sniffing it, and then dropping it in disgust.

Beau says, "Yuck! That's it!"

"Gross!" Millie says. "Whose jacket is this?"

The sheriff says, "I found it on the driveway across the road from where we found you, Beau."

Beau cringes and tucks her feet under herself and pushes as far away as she can while still gagging at the horrible smell.

"What's the matter?" comforts Millie.

"That smell. It's him," Beau chokes.

Rob asks, "Who?"

"Him! The monster! The shit-faced kidnapper!" she wails.

The sheriff says, "He's gone. He's not here. Take it easy! Calm down!"

"How can she calm down?" Millie says. "She's shaking. Let's throw it out the window."

Rob screeches to a stop, gets out, leaving his door open, opens the back door, grabs the coat, and takes it around to the trunk. He throws it into a box, then slams the trunk and dives back into his seat and pulls away.

Beau settles back into Millie's arms, whose eyes fiercely pierce the air, her firm grip now on Beau's hands with her right hand, her left arm encircling the frail girl in the fierce grasp of a mother bear.

"That's the smell I remember," Beau says. "Horrible, horrible!"

"I remember that coat on someone," Millie says. "I remember thinking it was too warm here for such a coat. Oh, my God! I think it's Ralph's coat! It can't be Ralph. Maybe someone else grabbed it! Someone capable of what he did to Beau!"

"Ralph likes me. It can't be him!" Beau says.

"Anything is possible," murmurs the sheriff.

"Could he be there, in the trees?" suggests Don. "Just watching us from behind them? Why would he leave his jacket there? It was cool this morning, but why there?"

The sheriff says, "Very strange behavior. Not normal. But in any case, this person isn't normal, whoever he is."

"Maybe he's hurt and might burn up in the fire," suggests Millie.

"Good!" Beau says. "I hope he burns alive!"

There is a shocked silence.

"We can't turn back," says Rob as his car bumps over the ruts in the driveway.

"Good!" Beau says.

"We hate him," Millie says. "But can we let him die if he's stranded there?"

"Yes!" Beau says.

"Fuck!" Don says. "Let's turn around," he says to Rob.

"You're out of your mind!" says Rob, but skids to a stop, reverses the car as the back end hangs over a cliff, and bumps back up the road as the smoke grows thicker.

When he gets the car back to the place where they found Beau, he turns it around so quickly that Millie knocks her head on the window. Rob jumps out as the car idles and leaves his door open. He disappears into the trees.

"Nobody here. Hello? Anybody here?" he yells.

No answer.

Suddenly, Ralph crashes into the driver's seat, half paralyzed, and pulls the car away, leaving the sheriff yelling and running after it.

"Ralph! What are you doing here still?" asks Millie.

"Wait for the sheriff!" commands Don, leaning over and grabbing the wheel.

"Not now. He can run down. I'm not well. I had a stroke!" Ralph speeds down the bumpy mountain road, knocking Don's hand off the wheel.

"You shouldn't be driving! What if you have another one and we all go off the cliff and die!" Millie yells. "Don! Grab it again!"

Ralph falls forward, breathing heavily.

Beau is hyperventilating and sniffing involuntarily at the same time.

He is her buddy. How can it be her buddy? Yet it is his jacket.

EVIDENCE

Ralph slumps over the wheel and passes out. His foot slides off the gas pedal. Don leans into Ralph's shoulder and stretches his leg over and jams his foot on the brake just short of the cliff. He yanks the steering wheel back towards the road and pulls on the handbrake with his other hand.

"I could strangle him now," Beau says as the car idles. Don switches off the engine.

Behind them, Rob is crashing down towards the car while Ralph remains unconscious. Don takes his foot off the brake.

"Shit!" he mumbles, grabbing his calf.

Suddenly Ralph comes to, grabs the key and switches the engine back on. The sheriff swings the driver's side door open and leans into Ralph with a straight-armed punch he'd learned in police school that he's never had to use once in all his years in the service. Blood spurts from Ralph's nose and he slides, feet first, outside the car by the sheriff's feet.

Rob drags Ralph to the back of the car while pressing his trunk key. The trunk opens up. "Is that your coat?" he says, pointing.

"Of course, it's my coat," confesses Ralph, holding his face.

"You did it!" Don splutters.

"Did what?"

"Kidnapped Beau!" Millie leans towards Ralph's face, frowning, restraining her wish to punch him as well.

"What the hell are you talking about?" Ralph splutters.

"Don't pretend. That was your coat," Millie says.

"My coat? I couldn't find it. I saw the back of someone leaving the living room in what looked like my coat. I figured he'd come back once he'd had a smoke."

"You mean it wasn't you?" Beau asks defiantly.

"I don't know what you're talking about. Wasn't me what?"

Don, Millie, and Beau look at the sheriff as he climbs back into the car. The silence while all their brains wrap around this statement is as deep as a well.

"Let's get to the hospital in Auburn," Rob says, opening the rear door and shoving Ralph inside, fingering his handcuffs. Ralph collapses and passes out. "I don't know what's going on. We just might have the wrong man."

Rob starts off down the gravel driveway and turns onto the paved road.

"Daddy! Help him!" Beau cries, reaching to touch Ralph's shoulder.

"You don't know if he is lying!" protests Rob.

There is another awful silence. Ralph comes to, groans and says, "I'm not lying. Why should I lie?"

"I know he wouldn't do that to me! We're buddies," says Beau.

"Let's get them both to the hospital!" Don says. "That jacket was the evidence. Ralph, what the hell were you doing way back in the trees? Hiding?"

"Hey, Don! Why would I be hiding? I think I went out to look for my jacket. It was dark. I couldn't see who it was. He didn't come right back inside. It just seemed strange and unusual. He should have asked me, just like people using my guitar."

Millie and Don mumbled, "Yeah."

"Later, I wandered out to find him. He wasn't on the deck. It was a beautiful sky, and I thought I'd go down the driveway. I saw a lump in the road, so I kept going. Just as I got near it, I began to feel very strange, I mean, like nothing ever before."

"That was your stroke, then," says Millie.

"Then my arm got numb, and my head was spinning. I couldn't even walk straight. I kept going sideways, and it wasn't down the road: I staggered into the trees and that's when it really hit me that I was actually having a seizure. Then I collapsed. I could hardly move. I couldn't speak. It was horrible. I'm so glad I can talk now."

Beau sits bolt upright as she takes all these words in. She still can't distinguish between that smelly coat and Ralph, sitting there, suffering.

"Can you use your arm now?" asks Don.

"I'm not sure I can play the guitar the way my arm feels. Damn it all!"

"Calm down," says Rob, speeding down the road, screeching at the corners. "We'll see what they can do at the hospital."

"Forget about me. What happened to you, Beau?" asks Ralph.

There is a silence as Beau tries to open her mouth. The smell of the jacket is still strong in her nostrils. She thinks it will never go away.

"Let her be, Ralph. She's had a bad time. We can talk about it later," Millie says.

Beau curls under Millie's arm and pulls herself into the smallest ball, like a tiny kitten. She can't talk. The idea makes her gag. She isn't sure if she believes Ralph, anyway. Maybe he is lying, caught by the fate of his stroke. At some level, she still feels like there is a seething red volcano in her stomach and that he is the kidnapper. She wants to climb into Millie's ample lap and disappear. The possibility of her own death has sneaked into her life too soon. The whole picture has changed. Beau wants to sleep forever.

THE HOSPITAL

The tension in the car is rising as Beau looks out at the animals scrambling uphill away from the smoke and encroaching fire. Rob must drive down towards it all to get out of there.

They reach the freeway and are speeding down to Auburn with the siren on and the lights flashing.

Ralph is groaning in the back with every bump in the road. Beau keeps pinching her lips together. Her lip is raw. She fiddles with Millie's fingers, squeezing hard.

"Ouch!" cries Millie. "Cool down, Beaudie!"

"Oh, I didn't realize I was doing that. I am just a mess right now, Mom."

"That's perfectly understandable. But leave my fingers alone. They're going to need to play the banjo when this is all over! You smell like a skunk!"

"I knew you were coming, Mom! I knew it!" Beau faints into Millie's arms.

"Quickly, Rob. She's fainted!"

Rob speeds up and they arrive at the Emergency entrance in only twenty minutes. There are other police cars flashing their lights, and the doctors and nurses are waiting at the Emergency entrance like nothing this exciting ever happens in this large country town. All the people in their trucks and cars from the party are there off to the side, as ordered by another policeman whom Rob had contacted.

Tiger races over to Beau as Millie helps her out of the car, and they hug briefly, but intensely. The musicians watch as Beau staggers into the hospital under Millie's arm, with Tiger helping on the other side. A male nurse helps Ralph out of the car and onto a gurney, which he then pushes towards the Emergency entrance.

"The police car escorted us down the freeway," Jim tells Martin. "Quite a sight. It was closed because of the fire, but they let us go down as the smoke wasn't too bad yet, so it was just us and them, like a parade of hippies for all to see. Everybody was tossing out their stash left and right. I'm going back later and turn around and cruise down in the slow lane to see what I can recover. I'll be set for years!"

"Hey, Beau! We love you!" shouts Moonbeam.

"Beau, take care! Out in no time!" yells Screwball.

"Did Ralph kidnap you?" yells Arnie, blowing his cigarette smoke up in the air.

Millie shoots him a mean look. "Leave her alone. She's in shock! No, of course, Ralph didn't do it! He had a stroke. Leave him out of this."

"Who did it then?" Squeaky yells.

"We don't know," Don says.

"That means we'll be here forever!" Gordon says.

"We have all your license plates and a list of your names," Rob says, bringing up the rear, just behind the nurses catering to Ralph on the gurney. "Stay here until you are all questioned."

Beau is settled into a wheelchair by a nurse and whisked towards the entrance.

Rob starts counting the people.

"Here's my list," says Millie, handing over her list of names.

"Again?" groans Jessie. "How long will that take?"

"Can we jam in the parking lot?" Misty asks.

Nobody answers. A look goes around the group, and like a school of fish, they all turn and run to their cars, trucks, and vans, and pull out their instruments.

"We'll serenade you guys out here!" yells Misty.

"Move away from the hospital. There! Over at the far corner of the parking lot," says the nurse with an air of authority.

The group breaks up into two: the blues lovers and the swing lovers. A double bass and a guitar player make their way to one far corner and the swing players follow. It is like the continuation of their party: all they can hear is their own rhythm, and their own favorites.

People look out of the hospital windows, moving as if they are tapping their feet.

"Beau's alive!" yells Arnie.

"Yay! Beau!"

"Love you, Beau!"

"You go, girl!"

"Let's keep her alive!" The two groups dive into the music they know Beau would love to hear and love to play.

"The night they drove old Dixie down, and all the bells were ringing…." sings one group.

"You're gonna miss me when I'm gone…" sings the other group.

"All it needs is a great fiddle part," Beau splutters to the doctor checking her heart.

On the other side of the hospital, Ralph opens his eyes. He can hear the music faintly. "That's the bit I like best!" His foot is almost tapping.

Beau smiles at the sounds echoing from the parking lot.

They all sing, "Michael Rode the Boat Ashore!" with Millie playing a banjo.

As soon as possible, Beau wants to get out of there. She will go straight back to San Francisco. In fact, she never wants to go to the Sierras again. Ever!

A MONTH LATER

"Mom, I'm just terrified to go home," Beau says from San Francisco into her phone.

"Whoever did it is gone, Beaudie. Long gone. This is the safest place you could come. But you probably have that stress thing…"

"Syndrome," Beau says.

"Yeah. Something stress syndrome."

"I am sure of it, Mom. I almost vomit even thinking about going back up there."

"What about Skyping? Kind of easing you back into the lovely scenery here?"

"Sure. But not right away. This works better for now."

"Okay. Ralph is here now and back to normal. Let's talk next week."

There was a long pause.

"Mom, no date yet. You don't realize what I've been through. If it weren't for you and Dad, I'd never go back there again."

"Okay, sweetie, poor thing. We'll talk later and see how it feels then. Remember, the fire never got near the Mansion."

"Okay, Mom. They still don't know who did it!"

"But they are working on it!"

"Gotta go! 'Bye Mom!"

They hang up. Beau chokes again, remembering the hole and the snake and being thrown over his shoulder and being left to die. No way can she ever go back, but she can't tell her parents. The Mansion was their safe haven; their new beginning from Oakland long ago just after she was born.

~❀~

Millie shuffles into the living room, still in her robe and slippers, and plunks herself down on the long, leather sofa and puts her feet up high on the back.

If she can't get Beau back up there, she wonders if she can even go on living there herself.

"Don!" she yells.

No answer.

"Don!" she yells louder.

She never yells for Don. Time stretches easily, not like a rubber band, but like a continuous, unwinding ball of yarn, she tells herself. No need to yell. He'll come back in for his second coffee soon enough!

"Don!" she screams.

"Who's dying?" he puffs in through the double doors from the deck.

"We have to talk!"

"We always talk. So, what's all this yelling all of a sudden?" Don comes over, sets his coffee cup on the side table, lifts up Millie's legs, sits down and lays her feet across his lap, just in front of his round belly.

"Beau's afraid to come back."

"That's understandable. Time will bury her trauma, won't it? It's just a matter of time."

"If she never comes back, I won't go on living here. Remember, part of the reason we stayed was to give this place to her one day so she could raise her family here, too?"

Don strokes Millie's shins.

"I never wanted to mention this, but maybe she won't want to raise her kids here."

Millie gives Don one of her eyebrow looks. He says, "What? You know I'm right!"

"I'm wondering now. She seems to have that post-traumatic stress syndrome! Ha! I remembered it!"

"That's going to be how it is, Millie. Let's hope it wears away."

Millie looks at the dust sparkling in the air through the sun's rays. She will never get this whole place dusted, plumped, painted and re-floored.

At least Gordon and Jessie, her unofficially adopted boys, have the sense to wipe their muddy boots before coming in, even in the summer. Well-trained boys: Millie likes that. Allen did a good job bringing them up. Millie is glad they use her house like it was their home. Maybe they will take over the place one day. Don and Millie once agreed that they could leave it to Beau with the provision that certain long-term people could live out their lives on the land. But Millie wonders if the kidnapper is one of the people living there. She doesn't mention it to Don. She would have been shocked to know that Don is keeping that very thought to himself.

Desperate

For weeks, Beau's wrists and ankles ache no matter which way she sits or lies down. In order to fully recover, the doctor has ordered plenty of rest. She hopes that the monthly jam in Berkeley will be upon her just in time for her body to be back to normal.

But not her mind.

The police have not yet found the culprit. The police questioned her for hours. She questions herself every day for hours. Part of her wants the awful memory to go away, disappear into a cloud and evaporate. But the part of her that made her a great fiddle player, something like grit and a need for perfection, keeps her awake at night, going over and over her list of facts: the smell of smoke, the smell of chloroform, the brusque jerking around of her body. But one thing niggles at her. She cannot remember who was standing near her when she took that last sip and then almost lost consciousness. Flashes of memories of being dropped off his shoulders and pulled into that cold place, a blindfold over her eyes, someone's hand twisting her precious right bow arm in a way that could have threatened to take her out forever as a fiddle player. She remembers the flash of pain, and her inability to see the culprit's face as he held her twisted arm straight back.

She remembers the near silence as the kidnapper walked away and left her half-conscious and very alone.

But the culprit is at large. There was a chloroform kind of smell about him that Beau can never forget.

DADDY

After two months, Beau and Tiger drive back up Route 80 to spend the night with Don and Millie. It is the first time Beau can be persuaded to go back. Their gig in Tahoe is too good to turn down. Also, the sheriff wants to question her a little more. She doesn't want to remember. But she loves the Mansion, a place she's known all her life and the weight of the years wins over that horrible night. Whoever did it was probably back in the Bay Area and surely not liable to return the following year.

Still, Beau asks Tiger to pull over for a minute. She hyperventilates while she looks at the black, burned ground up the hill from that fire for five minutes, and then they drive on again.

"You're lucky!" says Tiger, turning off the freeway at Dutch Flat and taking a hard right up the dirt road.

"Lucky?" Beau splutters. "Lucky is when you are not kidnapped at all!" Her dark eyebrows turn in at the middle like they are a unibrow.

"No, Beau! You know what I mean!"

"Well, lucky isn't the way I'd describe it. Sometimes all this positive thinking makes me sick. Let's take a look at the elephant in the living room. I wasn't lucky! I was totally unlucky!"

Tiger squirms in the driver's seat, and looks at Beau sideways as she slinks down so low she can hardly see out of the windshield.

"Well, Beau, what I really mean is that I'm ecstatic that you're here and alive and well! That's okay, isn't it?"

"Who said I'm well? I'll never be the same. I'm a damaged person. I have traumatic stress syndrome — that's what the therapist called it. I feel like I am not normal and never will be again."

"I can't deny that you've changed!" mutters Tiger, pulling the wheel hard around the u-shaped corner.

"I'll say I've changed! I used to trust everybody like, I mean, everybody! Now I don't trust anybody! I mean anybody, including you!"

"Me?"

"You! Can you imagine what people said about you? I know nothing. Maybe you were in cahoots with Dad. Maybe…"

"Beau, you are paranoid, and not in a good way. You are really off your rocker right now!"

"Fine. I'm paranoid. I said I've changed. I am never going to trust anybody again."

They both sigh.

"Except Mom," adds Beau.

"Well, that's something," Tiger says, as he pulls up to the Mansion and parks the truck. He gets out. Beau jumps down onto the driveway. Tiger walks right up to her.

"Don't touch me!" Beau says as Tiger's face draws near her lips. He pulls away, his face distorted, his palms raised, his eyebrows pinched.

"Beau! What's up?" he asks.

"I don't know. I'm upset. I'm angry. Not at you, and not at men, so don't go there! Just anxious and feeling, I don't know, like protecting myself."

"From me? I love you! You love me still, right? You used to!"

"Oh, Tiger, I still love you, silly! But I need more time to be normal again. Can't you see that just by being here again, I am still traumatized?"

"Yeah. I get it. Sorry, Beau. I just thought a hug would be good for us both." Tiger sits on the shady side of the bench and looks up at Beau's face.

"Want to sit down?" he suggests, patting the bench.

"No. It's hot there."

Tiger moves over to the sunny part of the bench.

"No. I really need to be alone, Tiger. I just do," Beau says, only glancing at his face.

Tiger pulls out a cigarette and lights it. Beau says, "I hate that smoke!" and picks up her pace to the house.

"Beau," yells Millie, running towards them, arms outstretched. They hug forever.

"Hey, Mom! It's okay. Everything's fine. I'm fine, aren't I, Tiger?"

"She's fine," he lies.

"Come and have some popovers, just out of the outdoor oven!"

Beau and Millie walk arm in arm to the huge deck.

"God! Look who's here!" says Don, spreading his arms and hugging Beau.

"Dad!" said Beau.

"Who's your dad?" he asked, putting his hand on her shoulder.

"You will always be my daddy," she says and touches his fingers.

They rock together for a long time. There are no more words. He draws his palm across the top of Beau's head like a mother does to her newborn baby and checks her face.

"All is well, intact," he says. "Now we can eat!"

"What's going on with Tiger?" Millie whispers to Beau.

"Tiger's a jerk. Can't see beyond his nose. He will never understand what I went through. I don't totally trust him, Mom!"

"Tiger is fine. He was devastated. If ever someone could be trusted, it's Tiger. Now, you are still in shock, but give him a chance. He loves you!"

"Sure, he does. I've become a bitch, Mom. No more smiley face here."

"You never had that much of a smiley face before, anyway!"

Beau looks up at her mother and smiles a fake smile.

"Good!" says Millie. "A little stiff still but keep pretending and the muscles will remember and fall back into place. It'll happen!"

Beau likes her mom's way of seeing the world. She wishes she had that optimism, but obviously, she has her father's DNA and his subtle occasional brand of negativity. But she laughs a short laugh.

"Coffee?" Don says to Tiger as he appears at the door.

"I'll get it," Tiger says.

Beau looks at Don's fingers and deliberately keeps her eyes off Tiger.

"Coffee?" Tiger asks Beau.

She looks up, and in that moment, she still loves that man. "Why not?"

POT SMOKE

The sheriff arrives and walks up the wide wooden stairs to the deck. Millie brings out his coffee.

What more can Beau tell Rob? It is impossible to trace back through those last moments she could remember at the party. Beau can only remember that she had played well and played so fast she almost tripped over a case at one point. She tells Rob again that she remembers laughing at herself as she staggers around, yet feeling proud that she didn't miss a note. And then she remembers taking a sip of her drink. She remembered momentarily feeling that it tasted a little strange. But she shrugs and jams her fiddle against her chin and on she played. She hardly remembers walking outside. She can't remember if she had been alone, or if that monster was with her, or if he came up behind her and twisted her arm so badly she couldn't look back. She can't remember any voice. It all happened so quickly, she tells Rob, and she was in such a wobbly state she couldn't resist the attack.

"I think some footsteps approached me from behind as I was kneeling on all fours, trying to stand again. I think I must have fainted from the drugs and the pain."

Beau says that as she lay there tied up, she feared she might be killed, slowly, painfully.

"Think!" the sheriff says, his coffee cup dangling against the railing. The blue jays squawk up in the pines.

"I can't think any more!" she protests.

Rob says, "All right, Beau. You've done so well."

"She's done very well, I'd say!" Millie says.

"But we still have no idea who did this!" Don says.

"It wasn't Ralph!" Beau says. "But that jacket! I can't get that smell out of my life. I feel sick every time that smell comes into my nose!"

"When does that happen?" asks the sheriff, leaning towards Beau.

"All the time," she answers.

"Can you narrow it down?"

"Let me think." She sniffs.

"It seems to happen when people light up." She means pot, but she didn't want to say it.

"Pot or cigarettes?" Rob asks.

Beau hesitated. "Maybe both."

"Not cigarettes?" Millie asks.

"Both," Beau says, "both."

She wants to find the monster. He is still out there. He could come back and try again! She knows saying cigarette smoke will narrow the search, but for some reason she can't say the truth. Not that she suspects her dear Tiger. No. He loves her.

Millie carries more hot popovers and butter outside to the redwood table on the deck, a silent witness to generations of conversations.

RALPH

On Saturday afternoons, Millie usually has a regular, informal open house and early evening dinner for the people living on her land. It is a tradition that Jim had started from way back in the later hippie days.

For years, people have come and gone to the so-called Mansion, gotten older; died. Millie trusts them all. She trusts herself, so she projects goodness onto all comers. She doesn't mind long hair or earrings on guys. She looks for the twinkle in their eyes and finds a shyness that the hair covers up.

After breakfast, Beau takes out her fiddle and bow and Tiger takes out his guitar and they set to practicing what they already know so well. Beau's fingers fly up and down the fingerboard and her right arm saws at the fleeting notes. Tiger and she are perfect together. No one can touch that sound. When he plays high, she plays low. Between their glances, their love for music and for each other is physically palpable and a delight for the group's eyes and soul.

One by one, the others arrive, instruments in hand, eat breakfast and quietly join in. It happens every time like that. Millie takes up her banjo and all together they fire up the whole mountainside with music.

Beau places her bow onto her strings and lights into an Irish jig and after the first phrase they all chime in, Don and Martin on guitars, Jim and Ralph on their mandolins, Gordon on flute, and Millie on her old banjo.

After they play for two hours, the smell of chicken and veggie soup overpowers them and they all go inside and sit around the long table, talking and laughing.

It is a while before anybody says anything serious to break the festive mood, but George finally asks, "Did they find the guy?"

Millie and Don each give him a concerned look.

"Aw, never mind, Beau," he says. "We just wish you luck and a beautiful gig up there in Tahoe tomorrow!"

"That's okay, Mom. I'm alright now," Beau says. "No, they never found him," she says, turning to George.

There is slurping and chewing and appreciative mumbling sounds as they finish their hot soup.

"Ice cream sandwiches are in the freezer," says Millie. "Just get 'em yourselves." Trained as they are, each one brings a bowl in and rinses and washes up and sets it in the drainer.

One by one they take their ice cream sandwiches out to the shady part of the deck. It is cooling down now, but still hot enough for shade to be sought.

"Mom, I think I'll go up and take a nap," says Beau.

"Tiger going up?"

"Naw. He'll play on with the others. I need to think."

Millie looks at the crease between Beau's eyebrows. No, she is still traumatized, no matter her protestation.

Beau leaves her fiddle in the living room and goes upstairs to her octagonal bedroom. She flops down on the pink and white eiderdown and pulls out her iPhone. The reception is fine from that satellite she can always see through her window out there at night, sailing across a starry sky. She opens YouTube and goes back to the same old piece and stares at Ralph and the others gathered and playing behind her as she stands there on the stage in front of them, giving it her all. She has noticed that Ralph has recovered the use of his hands and voice, yet he looks sick to her. He hasn't changed one bit and wonders how long he will live at the rate he is going.

POOCHIE

As Beau lies on her bed, trying to forget, she thinks she hears their little, black long-haired dog, Poochie, growling by her side. She doesn't even remember that he'd followed her upstairs. He is just always by her side. She sits up. Where was Poochie that night? He would have found her for sure. He would have followed the person who kidnapped her. He would have snapped and growled at him. He would have smelled Beau's fear. Did he run away from the fire? She has never asked Millie. Millie never mentioned it. Beau checks her iPhone for messages. Poochie licks her arm.

"Good dog," she says, hugging this mutt who must be twelve years old by now, his snout white, his black eye patch fading into grey. "Where were you that night?"

Poochie licks her face. Beau gets up and they both descend the staircase, side-by-side.

"Mom!" yells Beau.

"What's up, Beaudie?"

"Mom, where was Poochie that night?"

Poochie jumps up on the couch and sits next to Millie and leans into her leg. Millie pats his head.

"He was here, right here."

"Are you sure?"

"Of course, I'm sure! I fed him earlier."

"Did he eat his food?"

Millie places her hand against her chin.

"Of course. At least, I think he did. I don't remember. He always does. I would have noticed."

"Why didn't he find me that night? He could have found me!"

"Damn. Now I remember how he was left in the basement with the wine. We got home, and he was whimpering. How'd he get locked up in there?"

"And why was he locked up in there?" chimes in Don, entering the living room from the double doors.

"Dad. Did you lock him away because he barks at harmonicas?"

"No. I completely spaced out his existence. But wouldn't he have barked when we were all leaving?"

"Maybe he did, but everybody was so worried about getting out they didn't hear him."

"I figured he probably took off down the mountain with all the deer running scared," says Millie. "And I was so freaked out about leaving you behind, I just didn't even remember him. Sorry, Poochie." Poochie licks her hand and nudges against her leg again.

"Let's go check out the basement," says Beau. The three of them start towards the inside basement door. It is ajar. The light is on.

"Hey!" Tiger says, from below.

"What are you doing?" Don says, a little suspiciously.

"Checkin' out your wine. I was going to ask you!"

"See anything strange in here?" Millie asks, and shivers as all three follow Poochie down the wooden staircase into the cool basement.

They walk around, checking the floor for clues, and Beau takes up her sniffing. It seems she can't help it anymore. It is like she has become part dog.

"That's it!" she exclaims.

"What?" they all say in unison.

"That chlorophyll smell or whatever it is! Oh, God, let me out of here!"

She leaps back up the steps two at a time and collapses on the kitchen floor.

"Water!" yells Millie to Tiger who crashes up after Beau.

"Air!" mumbles Beau.

"She's got post-traumatic stress syndrome!" whispers Tiger to Don, who comes right upstairs after him.

"What's going on?" Tiger whispers in Beau's ear.

"That was his smell. Why was it in the basement? Why was Poochie locked in the basement that night? Who knows where the key is kept?"

The four of them pause and try to list in their heads the many people who actually knew where the key is kept. Over the years, it must have been over a hundred who have been invited to go down there and pull out a good wine.

"Too many," moans Don.

"But it narrows it down," Millie says, "…down to the people who were here that night who knew where it was. I'll check my list again."

"Open the windows!" yells Beau. Tiger runs over and flings open the double windows and turns to see if it helps Beau.

"Thanks, Tiger. I feel better now. But that smell!"

Tiger sniffs to catch the smell. "I can't really smell it, Beau."

Millie wonders if she should tell the sheriff. She can't really smell it either.

Never Again

The next day, Tiger and Beau load up their instruments and climb into Beau's beat-up truck, an old Chevy from Grandpa Jim. Tiger got his engine training on it back when Beau was not even a driver, when he took the whole thing apart and put it back together. Now it runs like a bear is chasing it.

"Give 'em hell!" Millie says.

"It's all right, Mom. I'll be fine. I'm a grown-up now!" Beau says.

"You're my baby and always will be!" Millie says, still so relieved to see her Beau safe and alive.

Don brushes off his hands and wipes them on his jeans, then leans in and gives Beau a peck on her rosy cheek.

"Earn your money, Beau. Remember, times change. One moment they love you and the next they'll totally forget you."

"Cheerful encouragement, Dad!"

"I've been there, sweetie. You're the best in this country. But the audience is fickle and so is the music business. Play like it was your last gig, and enjoy the hell out of your amazing, God-given talent!"

"Yes, Dad! I love you, too!"

Tiger revs the engine, admiring its purr, and listens like a new father cocking his ear for his new baby's cry.

"Beautiful!" he murmurs.

Off they bump down the dirt driveway and down the mountain-side to the freeway.

"She'll be fine," Don says, turning back towards the house.

"You said that the night of the party."

"Well, in the end, she's fine. That was a fluke. It'll never happen again, so quit worrying."

Don pulls Millie by the hand and up to his chest and kisses her. His whiskers tickle Millie's soft cheek. There is a slightly scratchy pain that reminds her of how much she loves him, prickles and all. He pats her behind and they walk arm-in-arm back to the Mansion.

"I couldn't live here without you, Don. It's the truth. It's too lonely when you're gone."

"What? With all these woodchoppers comin' over for morning coffee?"

"Not the same."

"Well, I hope they don't pat your butt when I'm not looking!"

"Don't be ridiculous. One pat and they'd be outta here. Let's have more coffee."

"You read my mind. I just hope she'll be a hit."

"'Course she will. She'll have groupies meeting her the minute they drive up to the hotel."

"Not so comfortable about those groupies. She's got young men as well as women drooling over her, too. It's worrying."

"Hey, you're the one who said she'll be fine. Now," she says, opening the screen door, "let's have that coffee."

They make their way to their favorite chairs and Don pours two cups, adding two level teaspoons of white sugar.

"I read somewhere that sugar's not good for you," Millie says.

"Yeah. Shall I leave it out next time?"

"Not on your life. Add a little!" Millie leans forward and brushes her banjo playfully.

"She'll be fine," murmurs Don, stirring his muddy coffee. "Ah! Nice and sweet, like you!"

THE BERKELEY JAM

The jam is on an unseasonably cold day up in the Berkeley hills. The summer fog will not lift. Never discouraged by cool weather, jammers come, parking far up the narrow winding streets, walking up or down with guitar cases, banjo cases, and mandolin cases. Beau and Tiger put their cases in the designated bedroom and start playing in the garage. Beau warms up with a bright fiddle tune and Tiger falls right in as some watch and others leave to find their own corners. A hearty group stays out on the flagstone patio and hopes the fog will eventually lift.

A mandolin player joins in, and a harmonica player leans down from his chair and selects his *A* harmonica, cups his hands over his mouth and nose and closes his eyes. You could swear it was a clarinet as he wails like the opening of "Rhapsody in Blue." A man sits on a wooden box and begins to thump out a complicated beat. More guitarists pour in, and a bass guitarist leans in to smile at the harmonica player. The music goes on and on, each player taking a turn to show off his talent up and down the fretboard.

Beau plays until her fingers hurt. She slips away and goes into the lower garden next to the pottery studio. She has avoided jams for weeks, but this is her favorite spot where people seem to appreciate her talent enough to let her be the star she really is. Sometimes she feels she has outgrown all these jammers. But Beaudie loves the camaraderie and laughter. She loves the old people who had seen it all and bent down to offer her advice when she was younger. Usually, it was, "Don't give up your studies — you can't make a living in music." So, she stayed on in community college, studying Italian, French and sociology.

But right now, Beau needs a quiet moment. She won't drink anything, so nobody can spike her drink. The truth is, when more people arrive, she becomes more and more nervous. That last song she felt her bow hand shaking. Maybe it is too soon to be around these people. One of them might be her abductor. She sniffs. All clear. Once that jacket was gone, she didn't smell that chloroform smell again, except in the wine cellar, and now, this very minute when her hand can't contain the bow. It is a faint whiff, but it is unmistakable. She begins to shiver and shake. Her teeth chatter. The fog is suddenly dense. She works her way up the flagstones and past the shiny green ivy and back to the patio, then pushes into the kitchen doors. She keeps sniffing. Ahead of her and behind her a group of people are laughing at someone's joke. She smells brownies and spaghetti and the smell she hates disappears, but not from her mind. Has she imagined it?

Tiger is putting a glass of wine back on a table and she tries to catch his eye across the crowd. Finally, he notices her.

"Hey!" he says, working his way towards her anxious face.

"Need to go," she mutters, her nose involuntarily sniffing.

"Got it. I'll get the cases," he says.

Beau stands like a statue, her violin hanging by her side, and her jaw grinding. As she stands there, she sniffs and turns around, her eyes moving in slits, checking people near to her and then others who are playing hard and not even noticing her. The smell doesn't resurface, but Beau is wary. Tiger will be right back. Nothing can happen in three minutes.

Five minutes pass. He should have come back. Beau begins to hyperventilate as Jessie moves towards her. "You okay, Beau?"

"Not really," she responds.

He puts his hand on her arm and says, "Let's get away from this crowd."

"I told Tiger I'd meet him here."

"He'll find us," says Jessie.

"No, I'd rather wait. He'll be here in a minute."

"Okay, but you look weird."

"I am weird. It's that smell again."

"What smell?"

"Like chloroform; like that monster who grabbed me last month."

"Oh, you think he could be right here? He wouldn't dare show his face!"

"Probably planning his next kidnapping," Beau says and begins to shiver again. Her teeth click and chatter.

Jessie puts his arm around her and hugs her. People always hug her; something about being small must bring out their protective instincts. Beau doesn't usually mind—she's used to it. But this time it only makes her too alert, like a horse, wide-eyed and ready to run, and she shrugs him off.

"Not now, Jessie. I'm a bit of a mess still."

"No problem, Beau. I'll kill that guy if we ever find out who it is!"

"But where's Tiger?" Beau asks in a whisper.

"Should I go check?"

"Yes. That would help my nerves."

Jessie pats her back and takes off towards the front door and up a few steps towards the bedroom, full of empty guitar cases.

Beau looks around at the crowd. It feels like she is in another realm, like the fog is really a solid block between her and the others. She worries about its effect on her violin, and where Tiger went. She's waited ten minutes now, and it is time to find him. She pushes through the talkers, jokers, and players and into the front hallway and climbs a short flight of stairs, turns left and walks down the short hallway and up the steps into the bedroom where the cases are always kept. She investigates her secret corner where she'd put her case. It's gone. She knows then that Tiger's been there and is probably outside searching for her. She pushes her way back out the front door and through the crowd. The fog is lifting, and the predicted sun is hitting the patio where a large gathering now hovers under the umbrella. Tiger is nowhere.

THE SMELL

"Seen Tiger?" Beau asks David, who is not playing his mandolin at that moment.

"Yeah. I saw him when you two got here."

"No. I mean, like now?"

"Nope. Hey Gary! You seen which way Tiger went a minute ago?"

Gary shakes his head, and says, "Smoke?"

Of course, he's gone out back for a smoke with a buddy. But he promised he'd be right back. He knows she's feeling horrible. He wouldn't do that! But she says, "Oh, thanks," and makes her way back down the side of the house past the shiny green ivy. She peeks around the corner and doesn't see smoke or hear chatter. But she sees her fiddle case. She dashes over to it and reaches down to retrieve it. As she puts her hand on it she sees Tiger flat out under the bushes, looking half dead. At the same time, she feels a hand covering her face and mouth with a rag. Her eyes are wide when she sees who it is. She breathes in, starts to go limp, and drops her fiddle. But before she can scream, he quickly puts duct tape across her mouth, binding her wrists abruptly with the same tape. But this time, he doesn't blindfold her as he hastily slings her slight frame over his shoulder. The last thing she remembers is that smell of chloroform.

He hikes up the narrow side steps going up the opposite, secluded side of the house, which run between the house and a tall hedge. She is almost unconscious. He lunges past the driveway and the parked cars. He opens the back of his truck and sets her down.

"This time I've got you!" he says. "Lie down." He binds her limp legs with duct tape.

If she could, she might have at least yelled, "Fuck you!" but she remains mute, and on second thought, she will not give him the satisfaction of even a mumble. She knows this man so well. Why can't he just take her aside and tell her he wants to rape her or whatever he has in his warped mind? What is this kidnapping agenda? He ties a scarf around her drugged eyes.

Tiger will wake up and search for me. Is Tiger okay?

The doors slam and he starts the engine and the old truck bumps down the hill and away. She tries to imagine where they are going. The curves of the Berkeley road are familiar to her, and she memorizes them and tries to remember where she is. He drives straight down towards the bay and turns right onto the freeway. Then he turns right off the next exit. She is getting dizzy. Where are they now? Are they back on the freeway? Which direction are they going?

And then she knows: they are driving back to the Sierra ranch.

HEADED UP THE FREEWAY

Beau's body bumps on the thin mattress in the rear of the covered truck. In spite of herself, the chloroform knocks her out, and she falls asleep for a while. Then she wakes up, terrified, bouncing along this freeway she knows so well, until two-and-a-half hours later when the truck pulls off the freeway, turns right and then up the familiar hill towards the Mansion.

She is jolted by the bumps in the road; they are so familiar she can even predict the next one. But after the turnoff to her grandfather's, her parents' and her own childhood place, the bumps are new — above their house. Yes, that figures. He lives so nearby! The truck stops, and he opens the rear door and pulls her out by her feet. Beau can only mumble through the duct tape. Again, he puts her over his shoulder and walks for about five minutes, opens a lock, marches her inside some cold place and lowers her onto a soft bed. He takes off her blindfold, then walks over and closes the door, and apart from a sliver of light alongside the door, she is left in pitch blackness.

SIMPLICITY

Simplicity is elegance, he had heard sometime back in the past. High up on the hill, he has discouraged visitors on hot summer evenings from the climb. People just know. He doesn't like visitors.

Behind his cabin, the mountain stretches to the clouds. The hole in the earth that only began with an idea and a square shovel starts to grow into a real doorway propped up like a Greek temple with four-by-fours and a four-by-six dark green and brown, wooden lintel. Normally such a planner, he has decided to improvise like they do so often in California and see what happens. After all, five feet in he might have found a boulder larger than an RV. He hates disappointments. So, part of the plan in this one instance is not to plan, but just to dig. A giant mountain of dirt grows alongside the path where his full wheelbarrow moves it and it becomes almost a road where the dark, loose soil slides onto a lighter brown earth. It will become a garden of mountain shrubbery when the room is finished.

He keeps his designs in a stiff black artist's portfolio, his articles from *Consumer's Reports* about top ventilation options, the new, thickened wallboard in front of the straw bundles that would hold back the cold and damp on the other side of the walls. He doesn't dare think of how long this might take, but he starts, now that Beau is thirteen.

"I might learn classical violin someday," is all she had said all those years before on her thirteenth birthday, lighting the fire from an ember that had dwelt in his brain since her birth.

He buys his materials from hardware stores in Colfax and Roseville and often in Grass Valley and Nevada City. It will be perfect. There has to be a flush toilet of sorts, and a sink with hot and cold water. The day he dreams up the fake glass window, complete with mountain scenery, which she can pretend to gaze out of, is his best imaginary projection and he feels calm and proud. It is his quiet obsession, and he tells no one.

For protection from suspicion, every day he will slip out of his dirty overalls and into his regular clean jeans and clean white tee shirt.

"What have you been up to?" he is asked.

"Just making noise with my fiddle, that's all," he answers, in his clean pair of jeans.

His obsession overtakes him upon occasion, and he will stop digging, wipe the sweat off his brow and ask himself, "What in the world am I doing?"

But the answer never comes. He brushes the question away and knits his eyebrows, some other part of his mind conquering sanity, remembering his devastating failure at the violin.

CALIFORNIA

The boy begins to have nightmares. No sympathy emanates from his parents. He starts picking his toenails until they bleed. His navy-blue socks turn dark around the toes. The skin at his elbows breaks out and he can hardly stand not to scratch as he plays. His eyes begin to weep long after breakfast time. The boy visits the doctor and hides his toes but sticks his tongue out obediently. The doctor only gives him aspirin. Sometimes the boy can't breathe. He fears going outside in case he falls and breaks his bow arm. His pale complexion becomes transparent. As the years pass, he keeps up his lessons with the same professor, but without expectations. The threat of a performance diminishes, and he gets deep pleasure out of his practice, so he keeps on. He has the music repertoire to fit his genius: Vivaldi, Beethoven, Brahms, Bach, Mozart and more. But he might as well have been silent, as nobody ever hears a note besides his parents and his professor. Ever.

At school he slinks into the corners, deep into a book. Rubber bands hit him from nearby, but he doesn't look up or protest. It seems that the less he reacts, the more objects are catapulted his way until one day he rushes a prankster and punches him in the face. He is banished from school that day in disgrace.

He refuses to return to school, so he is taught by tutors at home, and so he withdraws into himself and begins a plan at age twelve to leave England and go as far west as he can go in the United States. Whenever he makes a plan, that is it; he never wavers. He gears his school courses, of the few he can choose from, towards California. He knows Spanish will be useful in California, so he learns Castilian Spanish, a poor second, but which the tutor knows. At least it is Spanish he can read. He listens to Celtic, bluegrass, jazz and folk music in the music stores and strums those chords on his guitar only when his parents are out. He has no friends, so his daily rebellion becomes the act of playing music his parents would frown upon. He enjoys the happy, dancing music that he produces. His keen ear steals the notes from listening at the music store and flows out of his bow the moment he is alone. This gives him a kind of happiness and he vows to find a music commune or community in California.

He is young and very talented. He learns where to go and play all over San Francisco and into Oakland and Berkeley. He meets Millie while he is playing in Union Square and becomes friends with their group. A new friend of Millie's, Ralph, whom he met in there after a local jam, has invited him up to the Sierras for the first annual jam of many to come.

It feels like a swarm of bees, the way they all decide to move up to the Sierras. The people in the Sierras are very friendly and open to his move: good fiddle players are precious. Right away they offer him a stake on the eighty acres further up the mountain from the Mansion.

He starts with a tent, his violin and his new, but rough-sounding steel stringed guitar. He picks up carpentry as he digs his foundation and buys wood for building his one-roomed cabin. He hauls his newly cut wood from further up on the property to his site to store for the winter. People don't mind his apparent need for privacy; he gives them theirs. That is how it works best there. Every weekend he ambles down the mountain to join the others with their banjos and harmonicas and American lyrics. He sings a few Irish songs he knows, and they love him. Talking much isn't required.

THE VIOLIN

Beau sits so long her bones ache. She sits and stares at this room with no windows except a large fake window with a phony scene of the distant mountains. Classical music is piped into the ceiling. It is soothing.

What is Uncle Martin doing to her? She thought he cared for her. Waiting is miserable. Her bottom lip quivers. She shivers and puts her hand on the cold wall, which reminds her she is underground. She gets up and tries the door handle again, shaking it, wiggling it, and pulling on the door. She backs up across this cell of a room and sits back down in her chair.

Her chair! Now she identifies her safety zone. A chair she has dented with her sitting posture. It is her only rock now. She understands nothing about fake windows and damp walls. She understands nothing about her clipped wings. Why is she confined like this? She sits again, mouth open, staring at a fiddle case he has placed on the table across the room. It has been one week now. She lies on the rug and begins her yoga routine, but the mysterious violin case remains closed.

Beau has nothing to do but worry and stare at that case. Why is she jailed here? She sits on the bed for ages, and then walks across the room, back and forth. She keeps doing all the yoga postures she can remember. She does breathing exercises. Breathing is life. She knows that. Not that she feels hopeful. No, more like she is bored, and bored thinking the same old repetitive thoughts: *What's he going to do to me? When?*

She finally walks over to the table, opens the case and looks at the beautiful violin, then takes it and the bow out and over to her bed, and sits down. The violin is really stunning.

Beau slides her hand over its shiny, smooth reddish brown, almost copper, curves in a loving gesture and slowly circles the neck. Pausing a moment, she then lifts it up and turns its body towards her chin and rests her chin on the chin rest and lets it stand there on its own without her left hand holding it up. Her neck muscles fall into a place of familiarity and her head turns automatically to the left, and her expression remains impassive, perhaps like the Mona Lisa. Her eyes close automatically and as she leans over, her right hand reaches for the bow. She sits up straight, tunes the violin gently, then places the bow on the E string, and begins a gentle wail, a cry of anguish from a high note yet climbing higher, getting louder, the sound opening like a flower, when at last she bows it back and forth, dangling on the emotion that pours out of that quivering scream, and then, with a jerk of her head, she pops into a blues song that everybody plays, and she imagines the guitars, banjos and harmonicas, and her friends are all there, making music, having fun; being in community.

After a few minutes, she plays a fine finale so the highest tone and her bow leap defiantly and decidedly from the last note. Perhaps it is her first smile in a week. She sighs and puts the fiddle and bow back into their places in the case and glances at them lovingly, closing the case. Then, head down, she walks back to her bed and lies down, turns her back to the table, and curls up, her tears fighting to stay behind her eyes.

She hears him coughing outside, just a short distance away. She hates the idea that he might have heard her playing.

He clears his throat from the other side of the door and makes a stamping noise with his feet, then slowly opens the door.

"Nice playing, Beau," he says.

Beau remains curled in a fetal position.

She hears him approaching the bed. She holds her breath, afraid to her bones that he is now going to rape her, steal her joy, toy with her longing for life and music and happiness. Her ears prick with intensity like a cat hearing his footsteps. She doesn't move a muscle. She can hardly breathe.

A rustling near the table lets her know he is lifting up the violin. She listens. There is the longest pause while she holds her breath once more. *Will he hit me with it?*

And just at that moment, she hears the most beautiful notes coming from that fiddle, and she recognizes the composer as Vivaldi. For the briefest millisecond, she wishes she could play like that. All her life she only remembers Uncle Martin fiddling with the others on those country songs, those bluegrass songs. Once, when she was very little, she thought she heard him play classical music like that, but she has never heard him once play a classical note again — until now.

"This is for you," he says, laying the violin on the table. A more beautiful instrument could never have been made. "It was given to me by my father in England," he says. "He got it from my grandfather."

She keeps her face hidden under her arm and visualizes its beauty. But she doesn't look up and although tempted to reach out again to this most beautiful instrument, with a sick feeling in her stomach, and even a raging desire to play it, she can't think about picking it up again.

POWER

Now Beau sits in a farthest corner of the room from him, her violin perched correctly under her young chin, as Martin has instructed. Her eyes are closed. Brahms pours from the speakers into the room. She settles the bow minutely above the open string, hardly touching it, and begins to play. The sound is a cry of sorrow, the classical vibration of the strings that are the lump in her throat, her imploding devastation, her crumbling and disappearing sense of her self, and her soaring accomplishment of the most soul-wrenching high notes, the low cello-like pleading, and then the light, unbelievably high note where listeners must stop breathing and contain the sound in their uplifted, protective arms.

At the other side of the room, Uncle Martin sits still, right hand thoughtfully under his now bearded chin. A part of Beau only wishes he might nod his approval even slightly, sitting there with his eyes closed, his ears catching every fraction of a second she presents him of an agonizing wait for the next note. Brahms would have nodded. But this man sits as still as an alert deer, his ear seeming an intrusive inch from the F-hole in her violin.

There is a pause, just before the highest, most plaintive, soft, and beautiful sound a mortal can play, and she grins viciously, not caring about the berating that might follow, while her bow jumps into a bluegrass lick that still remains in her bones no matter how Martin tries to kill it. She hates his dark beard. She imagines she can stab him with her bow and plays faster and laughs hysterically as he strides across the room towards her, his arm raised, her face defying him to destroy her, his very own creation. All she wants is bluegrass. All he wants is Vivaldi. She feels that, in a way, she is now close to the world's expert at both.

"Now, from the beginning," he says, his face stony, but backing away.

Beau feels triumphant. At last, their roles are sliding, gliding, wandering and searching—but changing.

The Weight of Angels

"I'm sorry," she says for the hundredth time, hating herself more each time, but unable to stop herself — self-preservation. She looks at her bow. "My fingernails are too long."

Martin takes out a pair of nail clippers from his pocket and walks over and cuts her ten fingernails, then retreats back to his chair.

"Again," he says calmly in that irritating English accent.

Beau picks up her bow and holds it just above the strings; her head held high, her chin pressed exactly as he has taught her. By now she has almost forgotten how she'd held it for folk music and her wonderful bluegrass. Now her mind has to center completely on Bach and Brahms and Vivaldi. If a hint of a little Celtic style steals into her work, she cringes, waiting for the frown. She wields her bow in honor of classical music to sound like that famous Russian violin player she once heard at Davies Symphony Hall in San Francisco with her class. Her eyebrows even mimic his way of showing mixed emotions where they seem to be lifted at the same time as creased, or sad at the same time as serene. This is her new persona. She can imagine herself talking with an English accent, not unlike Princess Diana or Camilla. In her bones she has become taller, more dignified; she feels grand, competent. When he praises her, she sighs, but holds back her relief by slightly nodding downwards, so he can hardly see her brown eyes hidden by her long, dark eyelashes.

She has been in this underground room for so long she has lost count of the days. At first, she carved out the days on the hidden side of her bedpost with her fingernails, but after three months she gives that up and forgets why she is doing it. Somehow, she now lives to play as if she is standing on the stage at Davies Symphony Hall, or Albert Hall in London. Her own fame as a fiddle player of note seems far away and silly. Now she is a serious violin player. Now she will rule the world, and they will adore her. Her Facebook ratings will break the Internet: he promises her that. And she smiles as she lowers her left elbow and closes her eyes, and listens to the orchestral recording yet again, ready to make her violin sing with those poignant high notes that can make her audience clear their throats of the hidden lump, as their hairs stand up on their scalps and they remember their mothers' caresses.

Beau imagines him nodding and raising his baton again and again. Now his beard is shaved off; he wears a black suit and tie. He looks like an Englishman, not a cowboy. He also closes his eyes. His ear seems alive to her every nuance. Even though she plays out of fear, her love for the new sounds he forces her to play, make her almost forget how she's been kidnapped for his purposes. Once she remembers her own desire to play classical. She knows about Stockholm syndrome from her history classes where you take on the values of your captors just to survive. She knows at some deep, dark level that is why she makes those notes carry the weight of angels with fragile wings. She loves every tone she brings from these strings and this bow and her own undeniable sensitivity to classical sounds.

By now, she has learned to push her thoughts of the past away. She loves Tiger, but he is, after all, a smoker, easier to brush off than her mom, who will be going out of her mind and searching for her forever. Her dad will be stoic and say she'll be found alive. But mostly, Beau has learned to live in the moment, to love the irresistible French cuisine her captor delights in serving her. But mostly, she lives for the hours of practice and the ears that listen for the sound that is going to be perfect.

After dinner, she flops down on her double bed and wraps her small self with the fluffy duvet. The room is girlish, decorated by this man who clearly has planned the kidnapping for months, if not years.

The lampshade is fluffy and pink. Everything in her small room is like an old-fashioned architect's vision of the bedroom Peter Pan flew into in London, complete with pink flowers and green leaves painted on the wall, a music stand, and reams of violin music carefully sorted into files next to the baby piano. In one corner there is a small washbasin and a toilet. The room is not at all like her octagonal rooftop bedroom with treetops all around and views down the mountain towards the southwest. No photos or paintings here remind her of that life. She finds the Amsterdam scenes he has hung up ironic and laughs cynically, thinking of Anne Frank writing so beautifully during her own captive state. Beau buries her face in the down pillow and wonders if she will die in this prison.

PAYBACK

Measuring the minute distances from a perfect tone to an almost perfect sound keeps Beau's mind occupied when her shoulder aches. Practicing her scales gives her brain a reason to dance, hum, move, and feel alive. To escape, she feels she will have to become almost the best violin player in the world. She will have to go out onto the stage and smile at her captor as she raises the bow to the breathless audience who has forgotten the long, dark-haired bluegrass fiddle playing diva on the Internet and leans forward to hear this classical, curly, newly blond, short-haired violin player they have heard so much about, whose beautiful ruby-red lips will stun them into a hypnotic trance.

She will look into his adoring eyes, right there below her in the front row, just behind the San Francisco Symphony Orchestra, and burst out into Celtic music that can only be heard so beautifully in Ireland. Day after day, Beau imagines this scene. She delights in visualizing the shock on his face, his hands slapping against his eyes when his dreams are shattered right in front of a huge audience and the television cameras. She will be sure to let him kiss her cheek before she goes to her dressing room to change into her provocative yet tasteful black dress that will hang all the way to the floor. She will wear flat shoes, not heels, so that she can play, standing exactly as she has practiced. Perhaps they will be running shoes in case he jumps on the stage to strangle her before they grab him.

Such a dream! Such payback! And then the guilt comes. What he's given to create her genius! Really, he's given his very life! He seems to even love her and for sure, he loves her musical abilities. She needs every ounce of his devotion. His endless, quiet nods give her the will to go on.

"And again," he says, and now she loves to hear his somber, yet approving voice. It is never quite perfect, but it is very good, perhaps excellent, because most of the time now, he encourages her just with the tone of his voice. If he doesn't say, "again," or he leaves a silence after she has done her very, very best, she fears for her soul, the verbal lashes like a whip that had not long ago made her stand tall, raise her head, close her eyes, and produce heaven in a quivering note. Could she ever have done that without his insistence, for all these months?

But the dream persists. She will teach herself to overcome her need for his approval. She will never forget him as he languishes in jail, but languish he will, if she ever gets out alive. Her art is to get to that most public of moments, and then kick off those shoes and dance and play Celtic like never before.

NOT A HINT

Poochie spends most of his life now twitching in the shade somewhere on one of the decks. When he growls, it is while he is asleep, and his legs seem to be running.

"Gettin' old now," sighs Millie. "He misses Beau."

"Come here, buddy," Don says, reaching and beckoning to the almost blind creature.

"It's too quiet around here," Millie says, turning a page of the *Sacramento Bee*.

"Don't complain!" Don bends down and lets Poochie lick his ears. Poochie is grey around his snout, and he doesn't run often, but once in a while he will take off after some animal intruder and shock the humans standing by. But his days of hunting are long gone, evaporating like steam from a coffee cup.

Don is just sitting back down at the table. Poochie sits next to him when suddenly he jumps up with half a bark and a deep growl. He lopes over to the open double doors and bares his teeth at the hidden source of his discontent.

"Hey! Poochie! What's the matter?" says a cheerful Martin, holding out his hand with a real bone in it.

Poochie sniffs the bone, then moves backwards and lowers his head, his remaining teeth showing.

"What's up? Here's your bone," Martin says.

Don and Millie are staring at an unusually animated Poochie.

"Poochie, come here!" Don says with a combination of love and Alpha authority. Poochie stands his ground, growling and stealing a glance at Don.

Millie gets up and goes to Poochie and grabs his collar.

"I hope he hasn't been bitten by a raccoon. Rabies is rampant this summer. Sorry, Martin." She leads Poochie back to her chair.

"Sit!" she commands.

"Just checking to see if there's any news of Beau yet," Martin says, brushing his boots on the mat, then entering.

"Not a hint," says Don. "Not one solitary hint! I'm gonna explode if something doesn't happen. It's been three fucking months!"

"Don! No need to keep swearing. We all feel the same," scolds Millie.

"Do we? Who is 'we'?" blurts Don. "Everybody else seems to have gone their own egocentric ways, even Tiger. The performance, the gig, fame, is what matters to them. I'll bet some are relieved at the lack of competition now. I really never want to see those damned musicians again!"

Martin says, "They are just being who they always were. I agree with you, Don, though. After those first few days, things went almost back to normal. The Internet goes on and her picture is still up there, but real people? Where are they now?"

"Back in the Bay Area, yodeling," says Millie.

Poochie begins growling again. Millie hits the top of his head. Poochie squeaks.

"Kind of temperamental today," says Martin. "Getting old. I sympathize!"

"Coffee?" Don asks.

"Never could refuse it. Millie makes the best coffee around here."

Millie says, "Thanks, go ahead."

Martin pours a large cup, as always, and comes to sit at their table.

Poochie gives out a low growl, and Millie hits his head again.

"If he can't improve his manners, we'll have to put him down. It's coming anyway," Don says.

"Not on my life!" Millie says.

Martin sips his coffee and smiles.

NOBODY KNEW

Martin cannot risk losing his temper: bad tempers are giveaways. Beau will think she is starting to win, feeling a crack in his determination, a moment to win his sympathy. A tantrum means he has feelings, that he is upset by a door opening to his vulnerabilities, his possible softening, and her moments, however short, of seeing a way out.

But Beau is so stubborn, with her slight smile under duress, her own ability to remain silent when most girls her age might cry and beg or bargain. Beau is hard to measure. He thought he knew her so well. He watched her grow up from a baby to a tree-climbing eight-year-old, to a small miracle of a musician at ten and a fiddle player who made those delicate low notes peel into a soul, whose high notes brought one to tears. And now she sits there, this one who can bring out every emotion in a person—solitary, meditative, unresponsive—not like her old carefree self.

He hardly knows where to begin. His fantasy is of a feisty young woman who might spit out obscenities, hit him, try to escape, and run at him when he opens her dungeon door. But he has opened it every day to bring food and water and she never runs towards him.

Of course, she could be depressed. He imagines her staring at her fiddle and bow but knows that now she hardly ever touches them. She eats little. She lies down a lot of the day. She won't look at him or smile or even be grateful for his company.

She is getting thinner. He has such dreams! Can't she see that? Where is that imaginative young girl who had confided to him at age thirteen that she really wanted to play classical, but felt obliged to play Celtic to please her parents and be one of the crowd? Surely, he can tap that longing by separating her from that group? He has read up on cults and how people become deprogrammed. He imagines himself as the great deprogrammer. How long will this go on? He brings her ice cream and cookies. He brings her hot chocolate at bedtime. He brings her flowers in a plastic vase. He even reads her poetry and brings in his own violin and plays Brahms and Tchaikovsky with precision.

"Maybe this will cheer you up," he says. He holds the violin under his chin and stands as far away from her as the room will allow and plays it for her again. Nobody in their musical group knows he can play classical violin. After all these years, he has kept his talent to himself. Perhaps he hopes she will break now, hearing his notes sing and hopefully penetrate her very soul, her hidden desire to do the same. But then she lowers her head, and he probably knows she has heard him, but he dare not close his eyes.

THE VERY BEST

All the promises are a sham; the fame and fortune; the Davies Symphony Hall, even the Albert Hall in London. *How could I have ever believed him? Martin lies about everything. And I built my dream of survival on these phony promises!*

"I'll never be that good," she says, easing the violin down by her side.

"Yes, you will; you are already. Just keep practicing!" he says, waving his hands to encourage her to continue.

"I'm tired of practicing. My arm hurts, my shoulder hurts, I have blisters here on my hand. I think you can practice too much!"

"Never! The best musicians in the world practice at least four hours a day for their whole lives."

"How do they have time for the rest of their lives? They would be traveling, flying, booking flights, arriving, playing a concert, then sleeping, then back at the airport for the next flight and somewhere in there, four hours practicing. I'm done. I don't want to be a famous classical fiddler!"

"First of all, say 'violinist,'" says Martin, re-crossing his legs royally. "It's too American to say fiddler. And secondly, you are going to be the very best, or you are never leaving here!" He frowns at her with those thick eyebrows.

She hates him and his ambition. He doesn't really care about her. There is something inside him that is warped, and she can never get out of him why he chose her. After all, she didn't even play classical! Now that she does, she muses, she really loves its variety and the sensitivity that had never been demanded of her when playing Celtic or even bluegrass. But there, in this informal music, the beat was everything plus the sense that she was very competent and fast: she stamps her feet a lot like Rory Block, just to prove it. It's a different world and much more fun socially. But intellectually, she loves to be stretched like a violin string to the exact pitch and to be challenged by every possibility in all those classical pieces.

"I am going to be the very best," she says automatically. *I am going to get out of here.* She raises her violin and bow, closes her eyes, and plays the most sensitive and stirring notes she can, and she again tries to lull him back into his dream that one day she will play on the biggest concert stages.

She opens her eyes. His are closed and his hands are swaying like a conductor. *He is now in my power. How long will it be before I am ready?* She feels like she is truly as good as the best right now. *Is he just leading me on? What is his real plan?*

After an hour, he gets up, says, "very good," and leaves, locking the door.

THE NIGHTGOWN

Beau can't help loving the eiderdown. Just the year before, Martin had given her a very flowery eiderdown, which she kept in her room at the Mansion. Now she sees he must have bought two identical ones. It is a little bit of home and comforts her like when Poochie buries his nose in the crook of her arm. She hates Martin, but the matching sheets and pillowcases are a garden divine, and she is, indeed, a small puppy snuggling under the covers for warmth and security. Even the pictures he has hung as carefully as an art museum director are lovingly placed such that she can imagine looking into the blue distances as if they were real windows.

Beau tosses the eiderdown off and feels the hint of the chill of an underground hideout; feels the cold walls that hold the light away from the glorious beams of sunlight directly above the ground. The battery-driven lights and heater fade in and out this morning, like a beam flashing from a distant boat at sea. What if the battery dies and she is left in the blackness of a bat's delight? She will hide under her covers for the lifetime of an ant, waiting for her captor to renew the battery. What if he dies, just drops down dead (which she wishes for often enough), and she is buried forever, expiring like an animal chained to its cruel destiny?

She tosses her slippers across the room towards her table, which is complete with a red and white checked tablecloth. It has stains on it now, each a notch measuring her time of imprisonment, a memory that drowns in the overlapping time of day and night, only measured by her longer hair and nails and by her strange understanding that her violin notes can now match the best Russian violinist. Just as she sits down, there is a familiar rustle outside the door and then a knock.

Beau says, "Come in."

"Hi, Beau. I brought you new pajamas," Martin says, holding a package out with one hand and slipping inside her room, while carefully shoving the door closed and locking it with the other.

As much as she wants new pajamas, a certain pride that holds her together like glue and makes her say, "I don't need them."

Refusal is her only power. Not smiling gratefully is next in line. Not eating is still a thought. Escape is impossible; not practicing is boring and deadly. Refusing has to be the badge of honor.

"Come on!" he pleads and tosses the package onto her eiderdown. She shrugs.

"Let me hear you play now," he says, sitting in his chair and crossing his legs.

Beau reaches for the violin and the bow, always ready, and closes her eyes like she is hypnotized, and allows the ancient music to flow into her body and out of the violin, while she is transported beyond to a real blue sky, chirping birds and the whistling sway of tall pines.

As usual, after an hour, he nods slightly, gets up and walks out, closing and locking the door behind him.

Beau lays her violin on the table and the bow next to it, and dives onto the bed, grabbing the package, tossing it across the room, and smashing it against the opposite wall.

BLUES

From the moment Martin arrives in California, thinking about his past life in England almost totally stops, like a train track that had abruptly ended.

But there are moments in that finished hidden room before Beau was there when he turned on the symphony piped into it from his nearby cabin and then closes himself inside and plays his violin with the music of his past. No one is looking or listening, so he can soar like an eagle, or a king, or a perfect person right through his body, opening all avenues to his genius, witnessing them like a father's pat on the back or a mother's kind glance. He can be the perfection his parents wanted to love and only then can he take his bows without fear. He imagines an audience of clapping hands and approving nods, and he takes his bows with no fear or anticipation of an awkward need to dash to the smallest room in the building.

But mostly, Martin forgets his past. He has work to do. Hiding his project has been harder than doing his project. His cabin is up a steep dirt road and hard to walk up to. It is too hot in the summer and too cold in the winter for intruders. He isn't particularly inviting on the subject of company and people just know him through his regular daily appearances at the Mansion.

Now, as she stands there, he looks over at his progeny, her perfection pleasing him thoroughly. She is his robot. She must do as he says. If she doesn't, he will be displeased. He knows she understands his rules, and it gives him great satisfaction to be in this peak of control. He never analyzes his actions. He hardly questions his morality. But his pride at her ability under his tutelage bursts with its own energy and satisfies a part of his brain that nothing else reaches.

And her eyes, almost always closed while she plays, might open sideways at him from under her eyelashes, but only at the end of a piece, and at that instant, he might nod. Or he might not. He sees her need grow and her need to be perfect, and as he witnesses her perfection, he feels like a tall, sturdy building, unshakable in any Californian earthquake.

As this tiny creature plays, he muses at her ability to create soul out of every note. He is sure Bach and Mozart would have been pleased and astonished at this girl's interpretation of their music. There is something in her notes that hints of blues, but before anyone could possibly have named it, it will have flown away, and they would be left puzzling at just exactly what is different in the way she plays.

PERFECTION

Martin slouches in his chair. Sometimes he feels like a sergeant, forcing her to practice like she is only meant to be on this earth to play classical music.

He gazes inward, his eyes half shut, and remembers his teacher back in Hampstead.

"Perfect," Professor Klimpt says to six-year-old Martin in his German accent. "Perfection is our only standard. Now, again, and again: perfect!"

And Martin practices until his little fingers bleed, until he collapses right in front of his stern mother and father, their arms folded, their faces serious. Their son is going to play at Royal Albert Hall. He'd better! Martin is perfect. All three of them sigh and look up as if to hear even better. At the end, his teacher says, "Ah! Perfect!" and Martin puts down his violin and bow as he hastily departs from the living room to the bathroom. That is the problem with being perfect! He can guarantee the beauty of his playing, but not the rumbling and jumbling of his stomach at the end of it.

Years later, it becomes clear to his parents that, however perfect their son is, he will never be able to acknowledge the applause before dashing off the stage to the restroom. Their depressed faces, as they pay the teacher after Martin's final lesson, are enough to catapult Martin into a deep depression with an eye on California and a wish never to have to please his parents again.

Part of him now remembers that. He feels a momentary shame to have become like his own great teacher—but worse—like his own parents!

"Again!" he says to Beau in a low voice. "Ah!" he adds, "Perfection!"

Beau opens her eyes as she lowers her violin and bow and takes a delicate bow.

"How do you feel?" he dares to ask.

"Like a genius!" she answers, spreading out her arms, violin in one hand, and her bow in the other.

"No, I mean, your stomach?"

"What's wrong with my stomach?" she responds, eyes wide, looking down.

A small, lopsided smile grows across Martin's face.

"Nothing at all. Nothing at all," he says, rubbing his palms together.

Beau puts her bow to her violin once again and runs off a Celtic jig and dances with her toes pointed around the room.

"Cut it out!" he says, frowning.

NOT A CARELESSLY PLUCKED STRING

Beau drags herself over to the table and stands like the earth is pulling her to it, looking at her violin case. She looks at her treasured violin. Even the case looks regal, its hinges gleaming with reflections of her lighted room. Her shoulders fall forward; her chin almost touches her chest. She doesn't know how long she stands there. Words file through her head like bad poetry, meaningless gibberish: too soft; too loud. She has heard about depression in some musicians and artists, how they can never be the perfection they aim for, yet how they have to let it all fly away during performances and click onto the automatic track they have spent a lifetime laying down, and hope that thousands of hours of practice will glue themselves together beyond the consciousness of the expectant crowd and soar into some other land of solid understanding born of endless daily endeavor.

Beau lifts her limp, right arm up and over her head and swings it around ten times forwards and ten times backwards. A light switches on in her head and she feels her dull body coming back to life; she feels the poetry that hangs above this stringed temptress enter her own desires and habits such that reaching again towards its neck is becoming a possibility again. She plucks a string, then she stands there, feeling the vibrations right up her arm and into her head. She knows she can make that string sing; make it not a carelessly plucked string, but a live being like a voice, singing deep into the soul of a calm listener.

The violin becomes part of her body: how it gets out of its case and underneath her chin, she does not consciously know, but there she stands, reaching for her bow, on automatic now, placing the bow on the plucked string and challenging herself to weep from the beauty she brings to this long, high pitched, yearning call.

Beau knows she is ready. But is he? Is he ready to let her go? She puts the violin and bow back into the case and slumps again into a kind of catatonic stance she can hardly will herself away from. She looks at her bed, her cozy eiderdown, her two chairs, her round table, her pictures, even the curtains for her fake window.

"I've got to get out of here!" she says aloud, and reaches back into the case, picks up the violin and bow, and plays a slow, poignant blues melody that she has never played or heard before.

Why Her?

Beau looks beyond Uncle Martin and around her room. To her it is a cage, and she is entombed. He has decorated it with care, obviously, but she isn't fooled. She is his prisoner. Uncle Martin has always been so caring. She has only good memories of him, showing her how to hold her fiddle with her elbow down and not sticking out like some fiddle players who played it up, down, across their knees, even behind their backs. He always seemed so interested in her progress. Part of her hates him, and part of her loves him. It is as if he has two personalities: caring and commandeering.

Beau's head is constantly full of ideas about ways to escape. The hole behind her bed is no good. The hole underneath the bed is packed with dirt and it is only a few feet into the side of the room. She doesn't know where the outside is, and she doesn't know where to begin. The smell of damp earth is going to give her away. Reversing her efforts, she scoops up the earth and packs it back into the hole and pats it hard, then pushes the head of the bed back in place. It makes her use muscles that seem almost dormant, like that snake on her neck. She winces at the memory. Her yoga keeps some of her muscles toned. One of her imaginings is to escape by running through the door as he opens it. She doubts his promises, but like

Scheherazade, she keeps practicing and playing all the pieces he asks her to learn to perfection. Perfection is hard work in this rather stale air that is pumped in from the ceiling. In her moments alone, she studies the air vent as she lies on her bed. The ceiling is full of hand painted stars, and the vent is round and disguised as the sun.

As he sits and watches her play her scales, she sees his face when she opens her eyes briefly. He is content; he is nodding approval at her perfection. Why does he care so much? He is a great Celtic fiddle player. He and she have played duets forever of the folkie kind. It had been fun, the stamping of their feet, almost dancing to the beat, the bending at the waist to emphasize some notes; the enthusiasm of both of them for years could not have produced this care and this mastery of perfection. It is the music. But why her? Why so mean the way he'd abducted her? Who had this man been, coming from England with his pretensions of being a Celtic and bluegrass whiz? Who is this person whose only happiness is to play his fiddle or hear her play, but only to perfection?

"Pick up the pace," he says.

She closes her eyes and doubles her pace, up and down the fingerboard, even adding vibrato at the top of each scale.

"Yes, that will do," he says. "Now, Brahms, please."

She holds her head perfectly and switches her mind to this new mood, takes a deep breath, and starts in. She can hear her own perfection. Part of her soars at the pleasure of the sound, but she also realizes that she has never, ever, heard anyone play this well. It is the purity of the moment that catches her unawares. It is the sound of the true voice of her violin that goes so deep into her soul that for a moment, knowing that she would never have accomplished this trailing from folk concert to folk concert with Tiger, she feels grateful that she has experienced this amazing satisfaction. For a split second, she is grateful to this obsessive abductor. For a moment, she almost loves him and forgets his bad side. But she hates him more.

"Now leave!" she commands when she finishes the piece.

Martin gets up and leaves, closing and locking the door without a sound. She stands on the spot in a state of perfection embroiled with fury. She flings herself onto her bed and falls into a deep sleep. She could never play better than that. Never.

CALL IT OFF

"Uncle Martin," Beau tries the next day, sitting across the room from him.

"Yes, Beaudie?" he says, crossing his legs in a regal fashion and leaning back thoughtfully, like some English lord.

"If we call this off, I will never say a word against you. I will say it was voluntary and...."

Uncle Martin chuckles. "Beau, you can't be serious! You are almost ready! Your playing is perfect! I could never back down now!"

Beau breathes into her weakened lungs and tries again. "Nothing will change. I am really ready now and we can have the concert just as planned. But let me go home and say it was my idea and you will not..." she hesitates.

"Not what?" Martin squints.

"Not...be disappointed in me," she lies. *Not go to jail!* She pictures him holding the prison bars, yelling that he'd been deceived.

"When I make a plan, Beaudie," he says, clearly not noticing her wince at his use of her nickname, "I stick to it like glue."

Beau sighs. Her energy level is not up to this pleading or bargaining, and she has not slept much the night before, trying to work out some way to alter his insane ideas.

"Can't we make a new plan?" she asks as brightly as she dares. He laughs again, this time with gusto.

"My dear Beaudie! There is no good reason to change course. We must sail on to our final victory!" Here he raises his hand and his eyes as if he were a figurehead on a sailboat.

His enthusiasm sickens Beau. She fears he will make her play right now, and she doesn't think she can remain as perfect as he requires. What will he do to her if she fails? This is the hundredth time she fears that possibility.

"I'm hungry!" she says.

"Right," he responds, getting up.

There is a long silence where she doesn't know if her survival depends on her raising her violin to play, or if not raising it will save her.

"I'll get your lunch," he says, walking to the door.

Can he tell that her energy level is waning? Can he see his dream withering before him?

PROMISE?

There is no longer a reason to play, to practice, to become a genius. *He is never going to let me out. He looks so old and bedraggled, even with his new goatee. How will anybody believe that I am so brilliant, as he insists? He has such a warped mind.*

Beau is tired of trying to figure him out. Yet after practicing until her fingers are sore, she will pull down a screen in her head full of scenarios. It is her movie time: she invents stories about everybody, but particularly Martin. She sees him with his goatee, his black bow tie garlanding his perfect white collar, and his tux trousers creased to a sharp edge. His hair is combed but slightly fluffy — what is left of it — and he has a hint of class left over from his British roots. And that accent! Maybe it's phony like everything else. Maybe he was born in Arkansas and left as a teenager and reinvented himself?

Hours disappear as Beau sucks her fingers in order to numb the ache in them. Her fierce and mad desire to explode through that door is surfacing again — that door where she desperately wants to cry to the world: *Help me, please!*

She can hear him coming. She can almost smell him as he approaches the dungeon. He said it was made of bailed hay and is soundproofed. She stretches her arm back over her head and feels

169

something crack softly in her spine. She breathes deeply for once, re-lieved that he is returning, wondering if it will be food or news. Will he change now and become the beast she knows he must be? *This plan to have me play Brahms, Bach and Mozart to the world is an extreme tease, and now when I am truly perfect, and feel like the genius he insists I am, is he going to turn on me and all my months of endeavor, and kill me or rape me?*

She wonders why she keeps coming back to that thought. Hasn't he been clear from the start? Maybe she's watched too many late-night movies when she should have been sleeping. But there were true stories out there, she knows, of really insane people who have no feelings for others' pain and agony. He is one of those, isn't he?

The door opens. His smile seems genuine. There is a moment of trust, a brief moment of camaraderie, a moment of pride and a mo-ment of conquest for them both. He looks at her almost like he is proud and ready for the concert of a lifetime. In that very moment of trust, he steps towards her and leaves the door ajar.

Beau stands up and keeps smiling back, then speeds past him just as his large hands reach out and grab her sweater and pull it off her shoulders. She violently shakes off the sleeve and pushes on past him and out the door. He spins around and begins to chase her.

"Wait!" he yells.

"Fuck you!" she yells back and sprints down, down, down the hill, through the menacing trees, towards the Mansion. She can hear him running after her. She feels weak and clumsy, but she runs at a pace she can hardly believe herself. Her foot catches on a hidden twig, and she crashes down so quickly she can hardly get her hands in front of her face. Her fingers smash onto a sharp stick and blood begins to spurt on her left hand, her violin treasure, her high notes; her qua-vering, shivering, entrancing notes that make a Brahms concerto her very own. He grabs her hair and falls onto her back.

"You fucker! Look what you've done!" She shoves her bloody hand into his face and smears his cheek red.

"You little shit!" he spits and grabs her hand and twists it behind her back.

"Fuck!" she yells. "You're breaking my arm: my fingers, my violin hand and…and your fantasy! You're killing everything you created, you jerk! Let me go! Stop it! It's killing me! HELP!" she screams as loudly as she can. He looks at her hand and her face and drops her arm, smashing his hand over her open mouth.

"Shut up, you stupid girl! Can't you see what you're doing? You are ready! I've arranged your debut! It's all set! Now, shut up!" He lifts his hand off her bewildered face. She licks her lips.

"Get off me!" she growls.

"You'll do it?" he begs.

"Get off me!"

"I promise you fame!"

"What if I don't care? I'm famous already!"

"Famous for the classical violin?"

"What if I don't care at all?"

"Ah, but you do!"

She starts to yell again. He puts his hand over her mouth.

"Famous!" he says. He rolls over onto the ground and lets his hand leave her mouth.

Her arm hurts. How can she ever play now? She will play to spite him. God, she hates him! But for now, she will pretend to placate him!

"I'll do it!" she says, gripping her injured hand.

"Promise?"

"Promise!"

They stand up and she brushes off the leaves and holds her bleeding hand in the air and says, "Look at my fingers!"

"It's in two weeks. They'll be fine."

"Two weeks?"

"You are ready right now!"

She holds up her fingers and looks at his worn face. They are both breathless. She leans down and puts her right hand on her knee, then spies a rock by her foot. In a flash, she grabs it, straightening her body so tall it hurts, and whacks him in the face.

He grabs his face. "Fuck!"

Beau drops the rock, turns downhill and races away.

"Help!" she yells. Her fingers sting and are swelling. She sucks the blood and then lifts her hand up while she runs, dodging every twig and rock instinctively, as the top of her distant octagonal bedroom comes into view.

He is up again and running just behind her, holding his face.

"I'll get you, you little fucker! That's gratitude for you!"

She hears his boots behind her, thumping through the dry leaves, closer and closer. She looks behind her: his hand stretches towards her. She wishes for scissors to cut off her flying hair.

"Beau! Wait!" he yells at the back of her head. "I'm your father!"

ABANDONED

"My father?" The words slam into her ear, but nothing can stop her feet, which fly over broken branches, crackling brown pinecones and a scampering squirrel. She runs—his footsteps, so close, crashing behind her. *Liar! You're a liar! Don's my father.*

He is gaining on her. She glances back and sees that he can almost reach out and touch her hair. She can hear his raspy voice; almost smell his tobacco breath. *He's no father! He's a monster!* She knows he can almost reach her: six inches back, maybe five.

Beau can feel the strain of her breathing and how she is weakened by her lack of exercise: her lungs are wheezy. She can hear the orchestra, the crescendo; her violin screaming its highest, purest scream, the drums and cymbals crashing and pounding like the galloping of two desperate humans. As the conductor raises his arms for the final, piercing note, Beau stops short, jumps sideways, sticks out her foot, and trips him.

Martin goes flying and falls onto his face.

Beau says, "Yes!" And then, "Oh, God!"

Now he is putting his hands on the ground and pushing himself up, his breathing loud and heavy. She turns and keeps running down the hill, leaping like a gazelle, knowing the way since her childhood forest explorations, knowing the angle of the sun, knowing the hissing of the wind, knowing the sound of the distant freeway. He is after her again. The crackle of his shoes on the pine needles is louder. Her heart is pounding, racing, thumping. Her lungs burn. At last, the roof of the house in the distance is in view again. She slows, coughing, struggling through her final steps, her escape: her freedom.

She feels his fingers grab her hair and pull her to the ground. Beau screams, "Help!" as he twists her right arm behind her back and puts his hand across her opened mouth. She bites his palm.

"Ow!" he yells.

Again, she screams a muffled scream.

Down at the house, Millie sits up straight.

"Don! Don! Did you hear something?" She leaps up and runs to the door, cocks her head and closes her eyes.

"What?" yells Don.

"Shhh. Listen!" she commands.

Martin swings his arm away from Beau's left arm and knocks her out cold. Her head falls forward, and he pulls her onto his back and struggles back up to his house, breathing heavily, one foot in front of the other, his face bleeding, his heart too evident in his chest, with his eyes focused and determined to get to her underground room before she revives.

Beau moans as he drops her on the floor inside her dungeon. He closes and locks the door and turns off the outside light switch, plunging her into darkness. She raises her hand to her pounding head as she slowly revives. It is so dark.

Now those tears that she has so furiously held back in the hole and in her months of recovery come gushing out of her eyes and soaking her arm. Her whole body shakes as she lies curled up, abandoned like a doe who circles the forest and her dying mother, lost and alone, her body's life ebbing and crumbling for lack of a caress, a caring look, a moment of recognition; a small lick of comfort from a mother deer that is now impossible.

Beau lies there that night, hovering between the will to live and the desire to die.

For two nights and three days she falls into some dark cavern of her mind which sends her soul down to the center of the earth; like a well, bubbling at the shallow bottom; dank, deep, with no way back. She slips on the gleaming wet stones of the wall of the well, grasping with her fingernails, but the descent into this moment is a long echo into the abyss.

Despair

Blackness only enters her eyes when Beau stops crying. At one point, she fixes her eyes on a sliver of light piercing through the door, and it becomes the only meaning in her dark misery. It is a bright star in a black existence. It is a place she could squeeze through, like a sheet of paper full of musical notes; it is a shred, however impossible, of hope. And yet, that night, it disappears into the darkness and Beau is lost in the silent grave, dizzy with no clues as to how to balance as she moves off the cold floor and over to her soft bed. It holds her as she continues her plunge into this bottomless pit, this slippery, slimy place of despair.

The idea of escape has now all but disappeared. Her body shakes as she pulls her eiderdown over her head and breathes in the warmth of her own breath.

Will he return? Will he open the door and let the flood of light back? Will he forget her like he did that first time? Has he forgotten her? She falls into a deep sleep that has no light cuing her to wake up or sending her back to sleep. She eternally waits for his appearance, or even now, easily imagined, her own death.

Something so deep down in her soul that it has hardly ever been experienced by her brain seems to come awake. She thinks it might be a cell so far into her brain that it links her back to her ancestors thousands of years before. It is even fainter than the sliver of daylight that is just coming into her eyes. But it grows: two cells talking to each other; now four. And into the coming dawn outside that is showing her that sliver of light, she sucks in the stale air. She blinks her crusty eyes and wiggles her feet. She stretches her right arm straight up into the darkness. Then she pushes her frail body into a sitting position. She breathes and breathes like the first animal that ever breathed as it surfaced from the primordial slime. *Mom! I am here! Mom!*

Footsteps! Crunch! Crunch. The sliver of light brightens.

She cringes and stands up. Her muscles are sore and fragile. The cold wall leads her hands and feet across the room and over to the table and the door. The sliver of light teases her sense of balance. As she reaches the table, she blindly pats it until she feels her violin case. She opens it and lifts it up to her chest, caressing that lovely violin as she had done secretly when he left it for her. She sadly remembers its beautiful copper color and its ancient history.

As she glides her hand across the door, she places her feet exactly where they would give her the most strength. She anticipates the light that might just penetrate her eyes violently when he opens the door. She stares at the sliver of light just to open her pupils a little.

The door is being unlocked and shoved opened just an inch. The light shoots into her eyes and she blinks and blinks at the blinding intrusion. And then, as the door opens more, she raises her beautiful violin high above her head and with every bit of her might, she yells as she smashes it into his face and again on his ear, and she hears it crack in two as he lunges forwards. He moans but is not knocked out. Her moment has arrived — her last chance. She squeezes through the small space that his staggering has created and runs. She runs and her ears hunt for the sounds of footsteps following her. Her eyes are burning.

Behind her, the gasping continues, but the pounding stops as he collapses on the ground. She runs on, down the side of the slope, through a shortcut over the hill and arrives at the back of the house, and up the back steps and around the vast redwood deck, into the back kitchen doors. She runs inside and collapses onto the floor.

"Mom! Dad!"

ARE YOU MY FATHER?

"Don," screams Millie. "She's here!"

Millie leaps off the couch near the kitchen opening, and runs to her daughter, crouching down, and lifting Beau's head, then drawing Beau to her heart.

"My baby, my baby!" she cries.

Don comes running in, "Oh, my God!"

"Don, get cold water!"

"Okay, okay!" he says, fumbling with a green plastic water glass on the drain, filling it with water.

"Mom, Dad," mumbles Beau, opening her eyes.

"Water, Beau. Drink water," Don says, holding the glass to her lips. She sips and then gulps the cold mountain water.

"Can you stand up, Beau?" asks Millie.

"I'll try."

"Take it slowly," Millie says. They both pull her up and put her arms over their shoulders and walk her into the vast living room. They all walk over to the couch and sit down.

Ralph comes rushing into the room with a lit cigarette. "What's all the fuss? Beau! You're home! My God! You're so thin!"

"Dad," Beau says, coughing and ignoring Ralph and his cigarette, her unblinking eyes penetrating Don's armor. "Are you my father?"

"Of course I am! What are you talking about? Where have you been? Do you want something to eat? You look so thin! We are so relieved to see you. We thought…"

"Don, Honey, let her tell her story when she is ready."

"Dad," she says again, "are you my father?"

Don looks at Millie, bottom lip protruding, eyebrows raised.

"Of course, he's your father," Millie says.

Martin comes crashing into the room. "She's my daughter!"

All four faces turn towards this man they know so well.

"What the hell?" splutters Don.

Beau turns to Millie, "Mom?"

"Honey!" Millie exclaims.

"Tell them!" Martin commands.

"Don't be obnoxious!" Millie says to him. "Why are you out of breath?"

"Probably my heart," he says.

"What heart?" mumbles Beau, head down.

"What's going on here?" Don asks. "What happened to you?"

Beau looks at Martin. His eyes pierce her soul. Then Martin looks at Don.

"What's going on here?" Don asks again.

Beau runs out of the living room and up the stairs towards her old room. Confusion reigns. She can't put the pieces together. She hates Martin. But if he is her father, really her father, a whole new light falls on her whole horrible ordeal. She needs time.

"I'm never going to play music again!" she yells back down the stairs. Then a terrible fear enters her. Who is she without her fiddle, her stardom? Even now, who will she be without the story of her abduction? Nobody! No stage, no applause, no one taking a second look, even Tiger.

Where is Tiger? It has been months. He probably has a new star by his side by now. She doubts her own love for him now. If she never plays another note, their relationship will fizzle out with apologies:

no trips together, no times to be together, no laughing at the absurd-ity of their lives as a duo.

Even the idea of a fiddle makes her nauseous.

She goes into the bathroom and looks at her reflection. She is shocked! She hardly recognizes herself: her cheeks are gaunt; her eyes are hollow. Her hair is longer. She wipes her face and tears and opens her mouth wide and yells again; she screams, then she col-lapses onto the bath rug in a heap.

"Beau!" yells Don, clambering up the stairs and banging on the bathroom door.

"Go away!" she yells.

"Beau. Come out! Martin has left: had some urgent appointment."

"I bet he did!"

"Beau?"

"Are you my father?" She sits up, her ears awaiting the words she now so longs to hear.

"Come out and we'll talk."

"About what, Dad?"

"Everything. We love you, baby. We missed you horribly. We want to hug you and hold you. We were heartbroken."

If he is not her dad, he wouldn't be heartbroken. But if Martin is her dad, maybe he is heartbroken. Her tears keep flowing, though her ear is pressed hard against the locked door.

Solemn Oath

Don sits at the table and dials Tiger surreptitiously on the old black phone. He is in Tahoe for two nights.

"She's back. Come right now!"

"I can't. I have a gig tonight! Oh, damn. Of course. I'm on my way right this minute. How is she?"

"Just come. She's really shaken."

They both finish the call without a further word.

"He's on his way," Don says.

"She's not with him, is she?" asks Millie.

"He didn't say," says Don.

"I hope he has the sense to leave her there. Worst that can happen is that Moonbeam goes on alone."

"We'll see," says Don. "Beau has to see him, that's all I know."

"Right," Millie says. "We won't say anything else. Just let him hug her. She's been away so long!" She wipes her eyes.

"He'll be here in an hour," says Don just for something to fill in the wait.

Martin has returned, having washed his face in the downstairs bathroom, drying his bleeding cheek with a paper towel and concentrating his gaze on the edge of Millie's cup. Had he glanced slightly upwards, he might have seen the crease in her brow, the puzzlement in her eyes, and the slump in her shoulders. The three of them now sit in a silence of knowing, a silence of betrayal and a silence of fear.

Then Don speaks. "We have to talk about this."

"No, we don't!" Millie says.

"She knows," Martin says.

"Thanks to you, big mouth!" Millie says.

They sit immobile, steeped in the knowledge that age brings, that the fewer the words, the better the outcome.

"We have to tell her," Don says.

"How dare you break our solemn oath?" Millie's penetrating eyes dare Martin to look her in the face.

"I had to," Martin mumbles, glancing up, catching the arrows of her glare.

"Nobody has to break a solemn oath! What makes you so different?" asked Millie, crossing her arms.

"You promised Millie," Don says.

"He promised you!" Millie says.

"He promised us both," Don says.

"Okay. What's going on, Martin?" asks Don, turning his chest accusingly towards Martin.

Just then Beau clatters down the stairs. "That's what I'd like to know!"

"Come on, honey. Sit down. We are so relieved to see you alive!" Millie jumps up and her arm encases Beau's shoulders like the wing of a mother bird. She aims Beau towards the couch and they both sit down as if in a dance.

Don leaps up also and is hovering above them until Millie says, "Sit down, Don. You're making me dizzy."

There is a silence that only lasts ten long seconds, long enough for each one to frame a question or a lie.

"We missed you so much!" says Millie, hugging Beau for a long moment.

"I missed you guys, too!"

"What's going on, then, with Martin?" tries Millie.

"Are you my father?" she asks Don yet again, turning her wide eyes towards him without blinking.

"Why are you asking him that?" interjects Millie, loosening her warm arm and opening a space for Beau to hold her own.

"Mom! Let Dad answer!"

"Of course, I'm your father! From the moment you were born, I held you in my arms and have taken care of you."

"I know you raised me as your own, Dad, but that isn't what I mean."

"I'm your...." protests Martin.

"Shut up!" asserts Millie with an elbow gesture aiming in Martin's direction and a mean look pouring into his face.

"Where have you been?" asks Don.

"Stop diverting my question! I need the truth. Now stop lying!"

"Honey," Millie begins.

"If you want the truth," Don says.

"I said I need the truth!"

"She needs the truth!" Martin echoes.

"Okay. I raised you from the moment you were born. Doesn't that make me your father?" Don asks.

"Cut it out. Whose sperm made me?" says Beau, raising her voice.

Don and Millie look over at Martin. Martin nods. Beau feels a sudden pain in her stomach.

She points at Martin. "That man is my father?"

"He shouldn't have told you. He swore he wouldn't," says Don.

"Guess he changed his mind!" Millie says, frowning at Martin.

"I had to tell her!" Martin pleads.

THE TRUTH IS

Don and Millie slump as they witness the bull turning into a cowering puppy, and the butterfly expanding her wings halfway across the room.

"And what right, father or no father, have you got to kidnap me, you awful, horrible bastard?" shouts Beau, hands on hips, cowering over the couch as Martin tries to avoid her large, blazing eyes. "What right have you got, you slimy jerk?"

Martin opens his palms.

"I don't care who you are. I'm a person. I have rights. I have a right to be treated well, to be loved no matter what, to play any kind of music I want!"

"Beaudie…" Martin begins.

"Forget that! I am not your Beaudie! I never was and I never will be! You should go to jail for twenty years for what you did! I am scarred for life! How dare you do that to me? You are one huge ego-maniac, not worth the clothes you stand up in. I'm calling the police!" She reaches into her pocket for her iPhone. It isn't there. She sees one that is exactly like hers on the table and leans over to the edge, grabs it, yanking it away from its plug, and taps in 911.

Millie shouts, "Beaudie…"

Beau gives Millie a look that slaps a thick bandage over her mother's mouth.

"Beau," interjects Don. "Calm down. You are right, but please don't call just yet!"

"It's ringing," she says.

"Stop, I beg of you, Beau!" says Millie. "I have to tell you the story first."

Don looks at her like she is going to tell the judge the very truth.

Beau hangs up. "Two minutes," she growls.

"Sit down first," begs Millie.

"One minute fifty-five seconds," she says, staring at the timer on the iPhone.

"It'll take longer than that," says Millie. Don and Martin shift in their seats and keep looking out at the trees.

"Alright. Ten minutes, Mom. That's it. If you don't agree with me, then you don't love me." Her eyes penetrate into Millie's soul as Millie gears up to spew out the long-hidden truth. Beau goes and sits across the room on a high bar stool, still holding the iPhone like it is a ticking bomb.

"Go," she commands and taps the timer button on the phone again.

"Beaudie. Here's the truth," Millie says, looking at Don and Martin like a resigned juror.

"The truth is…" she tries.

"Nine minutes," Beau says calmly.

"Martin is your father," Millie begins.

"I know that. So what?" says Beau, "Eight minutes and forty-five seconds."

"So, the truth is…"

"You said that three times!"

"I'm…."

"Yes?"

"I'm not your mother."

Only the creaking of the roof in the heat could be heard, as all four of them find interesting patterns on the rugs.

"Mom!"

"This is going to shock you, Beaudie, but you are insisting on the whole truth."

"Well, okay. So, who is my mother, *Mom*?"

Millie and Martin look at Don. Don's eyes plead for understanding.

"Dad?" she whispers, looking back and forth from Millie to Don and back.

"I am so sorry, Beau," says Don. "The truth is hard to tell you. You've seen it all over the television, but you don't realize it is in your own life. I now have to tell you that, yes, I used to be a woman," Don continues in a low, male voice. He takes out a tattered photo of himself as a woman from his wallet and shows it to Beau.

"No way!" says Beau, staring at his face, then her face in the photo, then his face.

"Hormones," Don says. "And an operation."

"Mom! Tell me he's joking!"

"We're not joking, Beau. I'm sorry we never told you, but it didn't seem necessary."

"So, wait a minute," Beau says, eyes wide, pointing them at Millie. "If *Donnie* here is my mother, and Martin is my father, who the hell are you?"

"I am you mother, of course!"

"But not biological, right?"

"Right."

"This is completely nuts!" Beau says. "I can't deal with it at all!"

"Then don't. We've been who we have been since you were born, so can't we just go on that way anyway, even though you know it now?" Millie pleads.

"I don't know. I need to process this insanity. I don't even know who I am now!"

"You are the very same person, and we are the very same people as we were five minutes ago," Don says. "It is just your perception that has changed. We all knew it, of course, but you didn't. We love you just the same. That will never change."

Beau stares at Don and squints her eyes. She feels like vomiting. She feels like crying. Her lips pinch together, and her breathing almost stops. She doesn't know what else to say. "Great! I have three parents all jumbled up and screwed around!" Before they can respond, she raises her voice and says, "Well, I've been studying classical violin and I am now quite a genius at it!"

They all stare at this out-of-context remark with open mouths, as if their hearing has tricked them. Martin looks immensely relieved.

"I'm going to play a concert in two weeks." She studies her sore fingers.

"What the hell are you talking about?" splutters Don.

"My real father taught me these past months. That's where I've been."

"What?" shouts Millie.

"Voluntarily?" asks Don.

There is a horrible silence that lasts six months and they all look wide-eyed at Beau.

"Yep!" she says, leaping up off the couch. "Voluntarily!"

NORMAL

But then Beau turns to Martin and says, "You are a sociopath! Or a psychopath! How can you think what you did to me was normal?"

"He's not normal, Beau," Don says.

"Hold your tongue, Donna!" Martin says.

"No," Millie says. "You've created chaos for our daughter. You are not normal."

"Oh, really! Then what are you?"

"This is about you. You are not normal!" shouts Millie.

"Not at all!" adds Don.

"For a start, you knew we were dying inside, wondering what had happened to Beau. 'We'll find her,' you said! Hypocrite!"

"Well, I knew we would find her eventually, didn't I?"

"And you left her to die when we were evacuating because of the fire! She would have died! What a madman you are!" Don shouts. "I put up with you all these years to honor Beau. But now you're not even our friend. That's over. We can never trust you again. We should call the police right now!" Don glances over at the house phone.

"Millie, you got to parent my child. My child! I did not!" Martin says.

"But you got to see her grow up, Uncle Martin!" Millie shouts back.

"You broke our solemn oath!" Don shouts.

"I had to!" Martin yells.

"I had a right to know all this," interjects Beau. "You losers! Of course, he had to tell me! Why am I left out of this equation?"

"You were just a baby, so we couldn't tell you."

"I'm eighteen now. I bet legally I have a right to know!"

"Exactly!" Martin says.

Millie and Don bow their heads. "But this will mess you up for life now!" protests Millie.

"I'm already plenty messed up. I never knew who I really was anyway — just some progeny of you guys. Just something you can show off."

"We're proud of you, that's true," Don protests.

"I'm proud of you," Martin says.

Beau has a swift flashback of agonizing hours of perfection thrust upon her. "Now I am the darling of all of you: your ticket to heaven! Forget it! I think I'll take up marathon running. I think that's who I really am!"

Martin gently rubs his nose and cheek. "You don't have to do any more music if you truly feel that way. If you want the truth, I…wish my parents had let me go," he admits. "Sometimes I actually wanted to let you go. It's up to you now. You had the brilliance admittedly pushed onto you by your parents…"

"Yeah! All three of them! And who the hell are you to tell me what I can or can't do? That's over, you pathetic criminal!"

The three parents shrink like deflating balloons. Just then Tiger appears at the open front door. There is a long, thick silence as Tiger and Beau search each other's eyes. The cat can be heard purring, aloof on his pillow on the sunny window shelf. Poochie groans and turns over.

"Tiger!" Beau yells, rushing towards him with open arms.

His arms open like expanding tree limbs and enfold her small frame in an embrace of protection. Her head rests against his chest and he rocks her as the others look on in trepidation. When they part, Tiger holds her shoulders and looks at her, leans down and kisses her lips.

"Oh, Tiger, I missed you so much!"

"Beau, I think I have now died and gone to heaven! I can't believe you are here and alive!"

"Of course, I'm alive!"

"But we all thought…"

"I know. But here I am, in spite of Uncle Martin."

Tiger's eyes shoot towards Martin's bruised face.

"It was you!" Tiger says.

"He locked me up!" cries Beau.

"You pervert!" says Tiger, stepping towards Martin, fists at the ready.

"No Tiger! He's a sociopathic jerk, but he didn't touch me!"

"So, what's going on?"

"He taught me classical violin."

"He what?"

"I can play…"

"He held you captive to teach you classical violin? How screwed up is that? Couldn't you just ask her if you could teach her? And where did classical violin come in, anyway? I thought you were Celtic?"

"Martin's my father," Beau says.

"Oh, please! Don's your father!"

Don slowly shakes his head.

"And Don used to be Donna and is my mother. And Millie is nobody."

Tiger starts laughing. "Come on, Beau. You don't believe all this, do you?"

"It's true," Martin says.

"Don't talk to me, you snake," spits out Tiger.

"It is true," Don says.

Tiger steps back to Beau and holds out his hand. There is a slight hesitation before Beau places her hand in his.

"Come on, let's leave this crazy place. Come to Tahoe. Bring your fiddle."

"But…" says Martin.

"Shut up, you freak!" says Tiger.

"Tiger," protests Beau. "I'm not coming up."

"What the hell? Why not?"

"I need to sort some things out with these nutcases right now."

He soothingly drops her hand. "I understand. You need some time off from it all. I have a gig tonight but call me if you want to come back to San Francisco with me tomorrow. I'll sleep on the couch. Up to you. Moonbeam is up there playing clarinet."

"There's a jam next Saturday," whispers Don. "Just saying!" he adds.

Beau smiles at Tiger sideways as he leaves through the front door. They listen to his truck engine rev and hear him driving back down the driveway. Beau looks at the three of them in disgust.

Who is Normal?

"And you three, you can go to hell—all of you!" Beau says, as she texts Rob that she is up at the house.

Rob is cruising down the highway from Alta and hears the text ping. He swerves off at Dutch Flat and pulls over by the gas station. *Martin did it! Come now. Don't let on, though.*

Rob screeches up the dirt road ruining his car shocks. At last, at last, he will be able to handcuff this imposter. He doesn't put on his siren for the sake of her request, but his pulse is racing so hard he thinks he might have to retire by the next day.

He bumps up the last leg of the road and with a hard left up their driveway he pulls alongside Millie's truck and jumps out, leaving the keys in.

He tears up the back steps but stops to listen before he knocks. He hears them all talking. Nobody is screaming. He decides to knock, and then walks in, as usual.

"Hi, all!" he says, looking upbeat.

"Rob!" says Don.

"You're here!" Beau says.

"Rob. Great to see you," Millie says, but she is unusually quiet, like someone counting rosary beads.

"Millie?" Rob says.

"Rob. Great to see you," Millie repeats, but she doesn't offer him coffee, first time in twenty-five years.

"Beau?" Rob says.

"This family is one big mess!" Beau says to Rob.

"Every family is one big mess, Beau."

"Not yours!" counters Beau.

"Yes, mine. Especially mine. Sorry. But I've seen it all. Your family can be counted as pretty normal."

"You're joking! Do you know who Don really is?"

Rob checks with Don. Don nods and shrugs.

"Of course, I do! I used to date him — I mean — her!"

Beau's mouth opens wide. She steps backwards, hands on hips and shouts, "You what?"

"Before...."

"Now you're all sick!" Beau splutters, wiping her eyes and backing up more.

"No. We're normal. But obviously, we're honest. That's abnormal!" says Martin. "I've seen..."

"...it all!" parrots Beau. "It was Uncle Martin!"

"Martin, you are under arrest for abducting Beau." He pulls out his handcuffs while Martin backs away towards the double doors.

"No! He didn't abduct me!"

All faces stare at Beau, jaws agape.

"What?" yells Don.

"I went up there willingly to see if I could change who I am. After all, looks like all of you changed who you were!"

"Are," corrects Millie. "Willingly, Beau?"

"Yes," she lies, her eyes glaring at Martin.

Rob steps towards Martin, grabbing Martin's wrists, his handcuffs now around Martin's wrists. Habit overtakes the snail-like verbal debate.

"Take them off," Beau says.

Jaws open wider in astonishment.

Rob says, "But you said Martin did it!"

"Yes, I meant that Martin changed me. He changed everything about me."

"Beau!" Martin exclaims.

She shoots him a dirty look. "Now I hate the violin!" she says.

"Beau!" says Millie, Don, Martin, Ralph, and Rob in unison.

"I hate music. I hate you all, in league against me all these years!"

"No!" protests Rob. "You were a baby. And then…."

"And now I am eighteen. Work it out yourselves. Thanks, Dad," she says to Martin, and strides back towards the double doors.

Martin throws his cup on the floor, dashing it to pieces, and runs out of the room to the bathroom. They can all hear him vomiting.

It Won't Work

Beau looks at Martin as he staggers back into the living room: *Uncle Martin; Father Martin; just plain Martin.* Here stands a man who is as much a part of her life as are the pine trees and the blue jays. How can he be this maniac kidnapper and still be a man who stamps his foot with gusto and sings pretty darned good for his age? How long has he been digging out that huge hole and preparing for his pathological deed? It is true: she never would have agreed to take classical violin from him; never would have gone back to his house up the mountainside since she visited there at age ten. Yet he was part of the furniture. His laughter is pleasantly cynical. He is, after all, best of friends with Don! Or Donna! That explains their continued friendship—ex-lovers! *Yuck! Gross!*

Beau strides back inside and stands above them as they sit in their usual places at the kitchen table, and shoots glances at Don and Martin. Don has raised her from birth. She's never known another caring person like him. And suddenly here is a man claiming all paternal rights after smuggling her into a dungeon and making her learn classical violin.

She looks at Don's hurt and plaintive face. She looks at Martin's mortified expression.

Martin tries to crack a half smile when he catches her eye.

"It won't work!" Beau says.

Martin at least has the grace to look down and keep his mouth shut.

"I lied," Beau says in a low voice.

They all look harder at her trembling face. Since they are all liars, Beau decides to undo her lie. *This man is a crazy nutcase who plays great music. But crazy!*

"Rob," she says. "Get your handcuffs back out. Martin abducted me two times, scared the shit out of me, threatened my life, and bruised my body." She starts to cry. "The truth is, I am wounded to my very soul. He needs to rot in prison. Take him away." She turns to Martin. "You need to rot in prison!"

"You said, 'voluntarily!'" Don protests.

"Not voluntarily?" Millie asks.

Martin grimaces at Beau, then turns to run from the Mansion. Rob races after him, followed by the rest, out the double doors and down the wide wooden stairs towards the thick trees.

Rob pulls out his gun. "Stop or I'll shoot!" he yells, pointing his gun towards Martin. But Martin keeps running and melts into the trees. Rob takes aim and fires, mumbling, "Damn you, Martin!"

"Shit!" they all hear Martin say as he falls.

They run into the trees until they reach Martin. His calf is bleeding profusely.

Rob grabs Millie's damp dishtowel out of her hand and wraps Martin's leg, using a twig for a tourniquet.

"You are under arrest, Martin. You have the right…."

"Blah, blah, blah. Forget it. I know my rights!"

They all help Martin up and hobble with him back through the thick, dead, pine needles and the clean, dirt fire road to the house, walk him around it to the police car and see him settled into the seat. Rob puts on the handcuffs, then bandages Martin's wound, while Martin yells, "Ouch! Ouch! Ouch!"

"Martin, you will go to trial and definitely go to prison. Say good-bye!" Rob says.

They all back away. Their shocked faces each convey a lifelong relationship gone quite awry. Martin pleads with his eyes.

Beau turns away. "It serves you right! You're psychotic. You're crazy!"

Rob gets in his side of the car and drives down the driveway with hardly a word.

The mood back in the living room is somber. Millie automatically makes coffee and then the level of conversation rapidly speeds up.

"I never suspected him," Millie says.

"I had my suspicions," Don says.

"He was always a bit off the charts," Ralph says. "But hard to really see this coming. Hey, Beau," he adds, putting his arm around her. "You are alive and we're gonna be with you all the way."

"Thanks, Ralph. I need all the help I can get!"

Beau takes out her phone. She taps in Tiger's number.

"I'm driving up now. Is David there?" she asks.

"Yep, he's here with Moonbeam," says Tiger.

Beau sighs. He may be a smoker, but Tiger is still hers.

"You know, I am horrified to finally know who everybody really is, but I'm out of here. I really have to go," Beau says, walking down the outdoor deck stairs over to her truck and climbing in. It has been months since she has driven. The keys are in it, as is the country custom. She turns it over. It purrs. Somebody, probably Don, has kept the battery alive. And there she sits, warming up the old engine until it is hot.

She sits looking at the Mansion and the view, and up the hill that she has just run down. Her gaze stretches far into the distance again, almost as far as the sea. She could get on a boat right now and disappear and begin a new life. She can really find out who she is: not some parents' pride, but who she really is, deep down in her DNA. Is there such a thing? She imagines all the new people she might meet, perhaps in Hawaii or even New Zealand. Yet she imagines herself borrowing a fiddle everywhere she goes and playing for an audience. She laughs. She doesn't really have to get on a boat or a plane. Not really.

What will make Martin really unhappy? First of all: no big concert, no stage, no video, no worshipers, no applause, no money, but most of all, no classical music.

She backs up her truck and shoots forwards, bumping down the familiar driveway for an hour's drive to Tahoe.

THE FOLLOWING SATURDAY

The musicians instantly pick up all their myriad instruments as Beau automatically places her fiddle under her chin. Not a note is plucked until she lifts her head and rests her bow above a string and begins an arpeggio never heard by these folkies, and then a communal breath opens up each mandolin, whistle, fiddle, guitar, bass, drum, and banjo. They are off down the familiar highway that resides in their brains from eons before, that changes them from individual egos into one full orchestra held together by tradition extending way back to the swaying of all mothers with babies in their arms, the drums of Africa, the dances of all children, and of Native Americans.

Beau launches into a Celtic jig interspersed with a little Brahms and then swings back to a blues and then to the Paganini theme from Beethoven. There is a serious, yet wry, look that shoots across her face as her befuddled parents lean forward, trying to claim their brand of influence.

Beau keeps the sounds emanating from her fiddle, slipping effortlessly from folk and Celtic to classical, and marches to her own music across the grand living room and out the open double doors. As she plays on the deck, hawks fly from their nests, distant dogs begin to howl, and the wind picks up the chimes, and clacks their bamboo and rings out their metal.

Ralph sucks at his cigarette and walks further out onto the deck, away from the double doors.

Don takes out a small pipe and nods at Ralph and shuffles further over to him, lights up and leans into Ralph's smoke.

Millie reaches over and picks up her banjo and with her keen ear, sounds out the theme from Paganini: first time ever played on a banjo.

The Trial

The courtroom is filled with all of Beau's fans and relatives and musical friends. The jury is half men and half women.

The judge comes in and finally starts the proceedings.

A mixture of sadness and relief sweeps over Beau as she strides up to the witness stand and begins to answer questions.

"Were you held against your will?" asks the prosecutor.

It seems that the whole courtroom is leaning towards her for the answer.

Of course, I was! What are you asking me that for?

"Sometimes…" she begins.

"Yes or no," instructs the judge quietly.

"Yes, then," she says, head nodding, eyes closed.

"Did he abduct you twice?"

"I don't know who the first one was, but he did it the second time. I saw him. I wasn't blindfolded then." Beau steals a glance at Martin whose eyes seem to penetrate her very soul.

"Can you state whether or not you felt this first abduction was also done by the defendant?"

"There was a smell of chloroform," mumbles Beau.

"Is this important?" asks the prosecutor.

"He was wearing a jacket with that smell. Nothing else smelled that horrible."

The people in the courtroom shift, as if almost smelling that odor.

"Was he wearing that jacket both times you were abducted?" asks the prosecutor.

Beau thinks for a moment, then says, "Well, actually, I don't think so."

"Then how do you know about his jacket?"

"The person who abducted me at the party smelled like chloroform," says Beau, "and the jacket smelled like chloroform when we found it that first time in the driveway."

"I see," says the prosecutor. "Was there anybody else who might have worn the jacket?"

Beau looks at the group of her friends sitting there with rapt attention, including Ralph, and says, "Yes. It was Uncle Ralph's jacket." There is a shocked sighing from the courtroom audience. "But he said somebody else wore it outside the previous night," she hurriedly adds.

"So, there are two suspects, then?" interjects the judge.

"No!" Beau almost shouts. "Uncle Ralph didn't do it!"

"Do you know that for a fact?" asks the judge, his eyes hard on her, his body leaning towards her as if to challenge her veracity.

"He said somebody was…"

"Hearsay!" proclaims Martin's lawyer.

"Sustained," mumbles the judge.

"Where was your Uncle Ralph while you were being abducted?"

"He had a stroke," Beau says.

"Where was he?" insists the judge.

"Across the driveway from where I was lying, in the trees," she answers, looking right at Ralph.

"So, he could have abducted you and then had a stroke?"

There is a long pause as the people in the court hold a communal breath.

"But he didn't…"

"But he could have?" says the prosecutor.

"No!" she shouts.

There is a pause while the judge rubs his chin. "We cannot accuse the defendant conclusively with this inadequate information. Therefore, we will absolve the defendant from the first charge of abduction based on conflicting and inadequate evidence."

The people gasp and whisper.

"Order!" commands the judge.

"Now, my dear," the prosecutor says. "The second time you were abducted, you saw the face of the defendant, and you can swear that he was the one who did it?"

"Of course! He had a maniacal look of satisfaction on his face. And he said, 'I've got you this time!'"

"Objection!" says Martin's lawyer.

"Objection overruled!" says the judge.

"Thank you, young woman. Please step down," says the judge.

After a long silence, the prosecutor says, "Call Martin Sandringham to the witness stand."

Martin limps across the room with his crutches and swings himself up onto the stand, swears an oath and sits down.

"Did you abduct Beau Reilly on the night of August 15th, 2010?" asks Beau's lawyer.

"It was for her own good!"

The courtroom audience moans.

"I'll take that as an affirmative," says the lawyer. "We are not here to try her. We are here to try you!"

"But I am her father!" Martin says, glaring at Millie.

"Order! Wait for the questions," commands the judge.

"I want a DNA test!" Martin shouts, thumping his crutch.

"It doesn't matter what you want, Mr. Sandringham," says the judge. "A DNA test is not required. You held this girl captive for months against her will!"

"It was wonderful!" Martin exclaims. A moan went around the courtroom audience again.

"Do you find now that you had made a terrible mistake in your actions with Beau?" asks the judge.

"Not at all," says Martin. "I have given her the life she might have had if I had been able to raise her as her father."

People start talking and moaning. There is a long pause as the judge searches his papers. "Order in the court!" he says.

The jury exits and returns within the hour.

The judge asks the jury if they think he is innocent or guilty.

The whole room leans towards the head juror as she says, "The jury finds Martin Sandringham guilty."

People nod and whisper to each other.

Then the judge straightens up and declares, "Martin Sandringham, the jury finds you guilty. However, it is clear to me that you are insane. You will be taken directly to a mental facility and be tested once again and be held there until you understand the harm that you caused this young lady by your insanity. If you are found to be sane, you will be imprisoned for ten years, at which point the court will reconsider your sanity. Case dismissed."

"I'm not insane!" Martin shouts, with his crutches held firmly, as they stand him up and lead him away. "I'm not bloody insane!" he yells at the doorway.

THE TALK

In a YouTube interview, Beau says she hates this insane man who has kidnapped her. But only to herself and Millie, does she confide the contradiction she feels that, at moments, she also still loves him.

"Can I love and hate someone at the same time?" Beau asks.

Millie gazes around their large living room and lets the question hang in the air like a soft, quivering high note of a violin, like a question that no human can ever answer honestly. But Beau tends to be all black and all white, so she longs for the answer from someone else. Yet Mille just sits there and then looks at her, not even hinting at an answer.

"Maybe I should just quit playing the violin?" Beau says for the hundredth time. She tried it for a month once and felt more depressed than she was with the eternal voice of Martin echoing over every note she played.

"How do you feel?"

"I feel fine," she always says to Millie, when asked.

Beau's large eyes stare at Millie. Beau still doesn't know how she feels.

"How do I feel?" she echoes.

Millie nods.

Beau hates the gulf of nothingness that is left hanging between them, but she has no real answer, no real way inside that question. She feels fine. Fine. But that doesn't appear to be acceptable to Millie who had gone through a lot of therapy when she was very young. Everybody feels fine: they all say so.

"How did you feel when you realized it was Martin the second time he abducted you?"

"Feel?" she asks.

"Were you shocked, upset, angry, horrified, saddened? What?"

Beau is grateful for the hints. It is exhausting trying to work it out. Only one of those words work for her.

"I guess I was pretty shocked. I had no idea. I thought he cared for me. I thought he loved me like an uncle."

"Yes, but this isn't about what he thought, Beau."

"Right."

There is a long, long silence as Beau pictures his face at the moment he slapped the chloroform cloth over her mouth.

"I felt devastated. I lost my uncle. I lost my faith in human beings. I lost everything, my music, my innocence, and my trust in friends. I feel completely…." Beau lowers her head into her palms and holds her breath. She breathes in tiny wafts of air until her lungs feel full and stuck, and then she begins bawling.

"Love is strange," says Millie, placing her arm around Beau, as they sit on the couch and watch the sunset.

"So, is this the Stockholm syndrome?" Beau muses.

"The Stockholm syndrome is about survival, not love. Love is open, Beau, and innocent and non-judgmental and caring."

"Well, I must have had the Stockholm syndrome then," says Beau.

"Exactly. If you clearly understand this, and your meditation can help, you will feel it rather than know it."

Beau closes her eyes. She is back in that girly dungeon, alone, left with only the yoga postures and a few yoga sayings and the St. Francis of Assisi prayer that she had once memorized.

"Where there is hatred, let me sow love," Beau murmurs. "Oh," Beau opens her eyes. Seeing Millie's eyes shut, and her head slightly bowed, Beau closes her eyes again and goes on, "For it is in giving that we receive, it is in pardoning that we are pardoned…." Here Beau opens her eyes wide again. "I'm not pardoning him! I'm not that much of a Stockholm syndrome fool!"

"You never have to see him again. He can't harm you."

"Yes, he could if they let him out!"

"He is crazy, Beau! Nuts! I hope they keep him there even if they test his sanity once in a while."

"Insanity!"

"Exactly!"

"Mom? Where is the line between sanity and insanity?" mumbles Beau. "I really don't know. I mean, all those years before he seemed perfectly normal!"

"And yet, for maybe five of them he was making concrete plans to abduct and imprison you and had a perfectly insane notion that you would perform classical music on your violin publicly after that. He clearly couldn't imagine the repercussions that he would inevitably suffer."

Beau looks at Millie. She is so wise. But then Beau has all those thoughts, too, wondering how Uncle Martin could imagine he would get away with what he'd done.

"That's the thing about psychopaths," says Millie.

"Is he a psychopath?" Beau asks.

"Mental illness comes in all varieties. It's hard to say what a person has. It can be a combination and really impossible to categorize. There's a line: on one side is sanity, and just a hair's breadth can tip the balance to insanity. It may go back to a person's childhood and the coping mechanisms they used to survive at the time. There's so much we don't understand. It's easy to label people, but almost impossible to get it exactly right."

"I thought I was going crazy in there, Mom. But I knew I had to get out or I would wither and die."

"And you got out! Beau, Love. You won! Your sanity remains and you used all your wits to survive. That is healthy behavior."

Beau looks into Millie's eyes. Her own choices were survival. They were "healthy behavior." Beau takes a deep breath and smiles like an innocent child.

TRUST

Tiger reaches his hand out to Beau with a tenderness she can't miss. She gives him her small hand and they begin to walk around the Mansion on a well-worn path. They don't look at each other. Beau can feel a wall inside her cracking. Yet it still holds strong. They walk around the house twice. The trees sway slightly in the breeze. The jays chirp. There is a lone white cloud above them, moving from west to east. After the second time they slow down at the large garage door that is big enough for tractors. Tiger then looks at Beau. She hesitates before she looks up at his questioning eyes, then says, "I do love you, Tiger."

They walk inside, over to their special corner and he lifts her onto the bed, cradling her softly, waiting for her to kiss him. She crumbles onto the bed; he sits next to her, then gathers Beau into his arms with the tenderness of mother. He pulls her onto his lap. She had once trusted Tiger. His warm hand is on the back of her head, he gently pulls her waiting lips closer. She closes her eyes. But he doesn't kiss her.

"Open your eyes, my love," he says. She opens her eyes, confused.
"May I kiss you?"

Beau thinks a million thoughts in one second: how she has so longed for this moment; how she has even suspected him of her abduction; how this kiss can lead to fantastic sex and how she might not be ready or able to trust him or any man enough, ever again. She likes the way he hesitates and doesn't take her for granted. She likes his eyes, with a combination of love and respect for whatever her answer might be. This is something new in him.

She raises her hand and pushes his eternal cowboy hat off his forehead, leans in towards him, and parts her lips slightly as if to invite him inside.

She stops one hair's distance before his lips, those lips that have been the ones she had once trusted wholeheartedly.

"Beau?"

Beau closes her eyes again and waits like a trusting child for the kiss that will inevitably lead back into their cocoon of bliss and trust. She can't believe it, but as he gently brushes his lips against hers, she tightens her arms around his familiar back and kisses him hard, inviting him again to be the man she loved on her eighteenth birthday.

STANDING OVATION

Millie, Don, and Ralph break down and visit Martin in the mental hospital after six months.

The authorities have finally let Martin play the violin for an hour a day with a guard standing nearby, keeping an eye on him. With the assurance that he need never play before a formal audience, Martin's music echoes through the hospital where the others stop their eternal babbling and cock their heads and recognize the man who creates such beautiful music.

Beau declines to perform a note of classical music for about a year. And then she begins to play a little classical and combines it with Celtic and bluegrass. Someone puts it on YouTube. There is an invitation on the Internet that intrigues her. Some agent invites her to play at Davies Symphony Hall. Can she come and play Celtic, bluegrass and Brahms? Her following is clamoring for this, their own musical interests encompassing everything available to them now on iTunes.

Time flies by until she is ready. The big performance night has Beau more nervous than anything she has ever done. She wears the exact dress she had dreamed of, but, of course, Martin is not there. This is real. This is no dream.

She walks out on to the stage to endless applause. She bows a little, lifts her violin, hesitates, and goes inwards. When she begins playing her new violin, she forgets everyone in the audience. She closes her eyes, and she is somewhere deep in her own mind. The notes are perfect. She is perfect!

At the end of her performance, Beau smiles to herself as she bends forward and takes her bow to the thunderous applause that goes on for five whole minutes. Ralph, Don, Millie, and Tiger, who have been sitting in a row just behind the orchestra and perhaps are making more noise than all of the rest of the audience, leap out of their seats, grab their instruments, file up the steps onto the stage and stand behind Beau. They all burst into their favorite, blisteringly fast bluegrass piece. People in the audience jump up and clap and some start dancing something resembling an Irish jig.

When, at last, the music ends and they take their bows, there is a standing ovation! Encores! Flowers! Handshakes! *FAME!*

Beau places her violin in the stand, looks at the huge, happy audience, and lays her palms together in a yogic prayer position, and, along with her family and Tiger, bows again to the gigantic circle of standing, applauding, whistling and yelling fans.

THE END

ABOUT THE AUTHOR

Wendy Bartlett currently lives in Berkeley, California. She lived in England for thirteen years and visits her family regularly where she haunts the places she writes about like the Old Bailey, the River Thames and Rottingdean. She re-published her novel *Broad Reach* in 2019 and has published four children's books recently, including the popular children's novel: *The Flood.* The new edition of *Cellini's Revenge, The Mystery of the Silver Cups, Book 1* was published in 2020, followed soon after by *Book 2,* and now *Book 3,* the last of the trilogy, is done and published in 2021.

Derived from her screenplay, *Girl with a Violin,* published as an audiobook, as well as paperback and ebook editions, is her latest novel.

Wendy has written much poetry and nine books. She is excited to work on her writing every day, telling great stories.

The Elizabeth Books
Written and Illustrated by Wendy Bartlett

A beautifully illustrated book for children attending pre-school showing all the activities children do in preschool: meeting new friends, listening to stories, swinging on the tire swing, playing table games, singing with a guitar, hammering, riding bikes, and playing in the sand. Teachers, parents, and children will love this book because they can point and say, "We go to a school like that!"

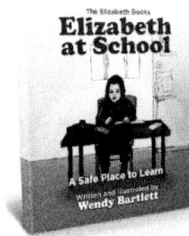

First grade is a challenge with new friends, maybe a new teacher and a feeling of advancement into the world of reading and writing. It is a time of friendship, sharing, learning and playing. It is a place where children come into their own, a secure leap into the world of math and science, and the beginning of learning to spell and sound out whole sentences. It is fun!

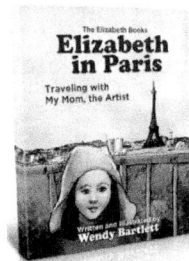

My mother sketches me all over Paris, whether of me eating an ice cream cone under the Eiffel Tower, or washing socks in the bidet, or going on the merry-go-round. It is lots of fun being her model! It takes many turns for me on the merry-go-round for her to finish her drawing. I don't mind a bit! Paris is amazing!

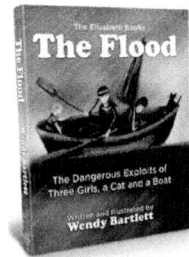

When eleven-year-old Elizabeth is left to babysit her four-year-old sister one rainy night, neither of them expect the adventure that unfolds. Their parents don't return home, and by morning there is a flood that fills the first floor of their house. Elizabeth must take initiative and make an agonizing decision: whether to stay put where her parents might find them, or to be brave and leave home to go in search of their parents. Dangers loom in either scenario.

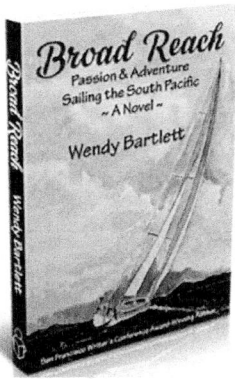

With her only child off to college, Sarah, a divorcée, is overwhelmed with emptiness. Here home overlooking San Francisco Bay is quiet, and her work with young children is routine. Most of all, her heart has become an excruciating vacuum.

When she meets a very sexy and charming Englishman tending his sailboat, Sarah makes an impulsive decision. It takes little to persuade her to join this mysterious sailor for an around-the-world cruise as his second mate, despite her amateur knowledge of sailing.

At first, warm winds, lust, and romance fill her days as they journey to the South Pacific. Soon her romantic idyll is rocked by the stormy seas as the dark side of her captain is revealed against the harsh backdrop of sailing. As life on the water becomes unforgiving, Sarah finds herself plunged into an abyss of fear and confusion, and ultimately, the greatest challenge she has ever faced.

Broad Reach is engaging, real and powerful. While most sailing stories romanticize the experience, this gripping novel explores the hard, cold, nitty-gritty, crazy-making, dark side of small-boat ocean cruising. A must read!

—William McGinnis, author of *Slay the Dragon, Whitewater: A Thriller, Gold Bay, Sailing the Greek Islands, The Guide's Guide, Whitewater Rafting* and more.

Cellini's Revenge

A Trilogy

"I loved this trilogy and appreciated Bartlett's invitation to do a review as I am an older reader who, until recently, avoided fiction, but have loved the limited fiction to which I have become exposed. I guess these characters aren't real, but they quickly became real to me, like a friend or neighbor who experienced a very different physical, political, and cultural environment. The genealogy of the extended family was a softer, non-judgmental version of *Peyton Place*, with the continuing underlying mystery of the cups and Cellini's curse.

"I loved being able to take my time checking in with these characters who became my friends across the sea in Europe. Book Three, as well as the others, fit into my "good find" category, not only easy reading, but the kind you can readily pick up and put down, knowing your friends will be there when you get back - no hurry - you can pick me up and put me down without missing a beat or the intensity of the story. I was really sad when I realized I was done with this Alfred Hitchcock mystery of mysteries.

"A few men have asked me how their gender is represented. My response: Bartlett has done a wonderful non-judgmental portrayal of the single parent family with the parent being a father. Being the product of a single parent family with my own father, Bartlett's presentation of small-town men was 'warmly' real to me.

"Bartlett's description of relationships and the twist they can take, is so real one wants to read on or fall off a chair. I was sorry to say goodbye but will always remember the Cellini's cups, the world they came from and the world of the Evans family, from a small, English seaside town, and their exposure to those cups and how the cups impacted their lives. It was a good read. I recommend it for both young readers and older adults. Thank you, Wendy Bartlett, for adding your voice to my family library.

—Peggy Newgarden, PhD,
University of Southern California, 1975

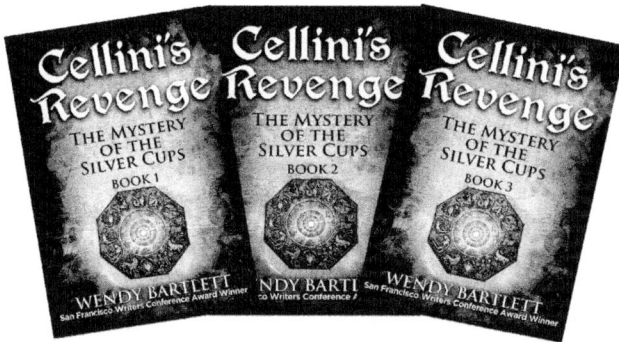

All of Wendy's books are available through Indiebound.org, bookshop.org, Apple Books, Nook, and Kobo as well as Amazon and other print and ebook retailers worldwide.

BOOK CLUB QUESTIONS

1. Which character did you think was the most believable?

2. What did each kind of music represent to you: Celtic/folk and classical?

3. Was Martin believable?

4. Could you imagine the surroundings of the party and the mansion?

5. Were the musicians believable to you?

6. What role did social pressure play in this novel?

7. What did her room symbolize?

8. Which character did you like best?

LETTER TO MY READERS

Thank you very much for reading my novel, *Girl with a Violin*.

I appreciate your interest and hope you found it as exciting and fun to read as it was to write.

I would so appreciate your taking a moment to please write to me at wendyberk@aol.com and let me know what you think.

If you would like, you could also write an honest review wherever you bought this book online, like Amazon. Here's a direct link to my author page on that site. amazon.com/author/wendybartlett. Just click on the black and yellow *Girl with a Violin* cover.

If you would like to be on the advance notice list for any of my future writings, please go to my website and sign up.

Thank you very much again for reading my novel.

Gratefully,

Wendy Bartlett

Wendy Bartlett, author
wendybartlett.com

Printed in Great Britain
by Amazon